The Shaurya Unbound

The Shaurya Unbound

Tales of Valour of the Central Reserve Police Force

Editors

Nitu • M. Dhinakaran

PRABHAT PRAKASHAN

Central Reserve Police Force

Published by
PRABHAT PRAKASHAN PVT. LTD.
4/19 Asaf Ali Road,
New Delhi-110002 (INDIA)
e-mail: prabhatbooks@gmail.com

for
CENTRAL RESERVE POLICE FORCE
Directorate General, CRPF
Block No.1, CGO Complex
Lodhi Road
New Delhi-110003

ISBN 978-93-90366-79-8
THE SHAURYA UNBOUND
Tales of Valour of CRPF
Ed. Nitu and M. Dhinakaran

Graphics
Amit

Edition
2025

Price
₹ 250.00 (Rupees Two Hundred Fifty only)

Printed at
R-Tech Offset Printers, Delhi

Dedicated to
the citizens of our country

डॉ. ए.पी. माहेश्वरी भा.पु.से.
Dr. A.P. Maheshwari IPS

महानिदेशक
केंद्रीय रिजर्व पुलिस बल
Director General
Central Reserve Police Force
Block-01, C.G.O. Complex,
Lodhi Road, New Delhi-110003
Tel: 011-24360971
Fax: 011-24363192
E-mail: dg@crpf.gov.in

Foreword

We are a nation that celebrates the valour of our heroes and holds the sacrifice of our Bravehearts sacred. Since its raising in 1939, the history of CRPF is replete with acts of exemplary grit and valour. These acts of bravery were adorned with gallantry medals of which CRPF has the honour of receiving the most among all Central Armed Police Forces. These stories embody courage, patriotism, integrity, discipline, and selfless devotion to duty. These true stories and the pride they bring is a heritage of each and every citizen of this country. And so like every heritage these acts of gallantry should reach every countryman. They will serve as guiding light for posterity and keep inspiring the generations to come.

This book that narrates the stories of Chakra awardees of CRPF is an attempt to bring the intricate details of gallant acts with valuable insights while also projecting the backdrop of the operations where these acts of valour took place. This book is written with reverence to bravery, adherence for accuracy, and most importantly a passion that simmers in the heart of a patriot.

A. P. Maheshwari
(Dr. A.P. Maheshwari)
Director General, CRPF
4. 12. 2020

The Gallant Force

The Central Reserve Police Force has the distinction of being the largest Paramilitary Force in the world. The troops fight insurgency and terrorism, quell communal riots and rush during natural calamities and disasters to provide the healing touch to the vulnerable sections of the society. A large footprint ensures that the personnel are spread across the length and breadth of the country. From the snow-clad Himalayas in the north to the rippling waters of Kanyakumari, from the sizzling deserts of Rajasthan to the lush green forests of the North-east, the country is full of diversity. We differ in language, attire, culture, cuisine and the weather varies to the extreme. And yet, the social fabric has held intact. It has been able to sustain the pressure that might come from the push and pull of the vagaries of such diversity. One organisation that has helped achieve this very difficult task is the Central Reserve Police Force. The federal structure of the Indian Constitution makes this Force uniquely capable of operating across all domains.

Raised as the Crown Representative's Police Force in 1939, post-Independence, its destiny had to be decided afresh. The decade old Force had proved its mettle and the sanguine Home Minister, Sardar Patel, the Iron man of India argued for the need of such a Force. Thus, the CRPF was retained and rechristened as the Central Reserve Police Force after a decade of its existence.

The last eight decades have been a saga of sacrifice and courage, of battles won and constant vigil to protect the unity and integrity of the country. There have been moments of extraordinary courage and valour; and also those moments of quiet remembrance and gratitude where we cherish and celebrate the memory of our martyrs who have made the Supreme sacrifice at the altar of duty.

The CRPF proudly holds the distinction of having the largest number of Gallantry Medals to its credit. An illustrious tally of George Cross–1, King's PMG–3, Ashok Chakra–1, Vir Chakra–1, Kirti Chakras–6, Shaurya Chakra–26, PPFSMG–49, President's Police Medal for Gallantry–200, Yudh Seva Medal–1, Sena Medal–5, Police Medal for Gallantry–1623, IPMG–05, the Force stands tall on the national horizon.

The book, 'The Shaurya Unbound', is about tales of our heroes. These are men and women who make us proud. Under adverse conditions where any normal person would wilt, some are able to stand tall and exhibit unflinching courage. These are leaders who have taken it upon themselves to lead by example and rise to the occasion. These are tales of what hones the steel in the person and separates the extraordinary from the ordinary.

These stories shall be presented in Volumes as we narrate the life-stories of our valiant warriors. It gives us immense pride to present the first book of the series. This book contains 13 stories of our gallant soldiers.

—Nitu • M. Dhinakaran

Contents

राष्ट्ररक्षासमं पुण्यं, राष्ट्ररक्षासमं व्रतम्,
राष्ट्ररक्षासमं यज्ञो, दृष्टो नैव च नैव च।।

There is nothing more sacred more virtuous or more important than National defence

Indomitable Courage

T. MOHANAN

As the passengers made their way through the portals at the Madras airport to complete the formalities, Mohanan took a deep breath. This was his first visit to an airport. Growing up in Keshvapuram, an urban area of Thiruvananthapuram, Mohanan had not imagined travelling in a plane. The eldest of five siblings, he found studies taxing. He wanted to read and explore, but the learning that he received at St. Mary's School, at Pattom, was too much for an inquisitive child like him. He had often looked with awe at the expanse of the skies and what lay beyond the city limits.

As his plane cruised over the Indian Ocean, he smiled. His desire of wanting to see the earth below from the sky was being fulfilled today. His father served in the Indian Army and was rarely home. It was left to the mother to bring up the energetic children. A childhood visit to the sea-beach on a rare vacation made him wonder at the enormity of the ocean. The scene was unfolding before him today.

Seventeen years ago, Mohanan had made up his mind to explore the world. Somehow, Thiruvananthapuram seemed too small a city. It was a bustling city and as the capital of the southern state of Kerala, it was the nerve centre for business and international diaspora. The city derives its name from the Malayalam word, *Thiru Anantha Puram* which literally means 'The City of Lord Ananta' which refers to the deity of the Sri PadmanabhaswamyTemple. His parents were deeply religious. Mohanan was convinced his destiny lay not in the city. One day, he just packed his bags and left the close confines of his home.

His parents heard from him a year later. He returned home as a smart young man. Gone was the uncertain and restless boy and instead there emerged a confident young man. Providence had taken him to a recruitment drive by the Central Reserve Police Force (CRPF). It was 1971 and he had enrolled with the 35 Bn CRPF which was then deployed at Dimapur, Nagaland. As he narrated his experiences with the CRPF, his mother realised that the CRPF was not just a profession or a job to him; it was a breathing entity. He had become passionate about the CRPF. His parents were genuinely glad and relieved. Mohanan married a local woman named Padmini on November 23, 1983. He was blessed with a daughter whom he named Beena. His second daughter, Nisha was born soon afterwards. Mohanan was very attached to his daughters and as he sat in the plane he thought of all the stories he would narrate to them on his return. He wanted them to grow up into confident women who would be able to see the world and explore across nations.

As the flight drew towards its destination, Mohanan thought of the flurry of activities that had preceded this flight. The company had been earmarked for moving to Sri

Lanka as part of the Indian Peace-Keeping Force or the IPKF, which was a first in many ways. For Mohanan, it actually meant being able to cross the seas. Sri Lanka, till now, had only meant a green emerald island suspended in the vast blue waters of the Indian Ocean. Of course, it had meant Ravana's abode too; now, it meant the place of his deployment.

The IPKF was the Indian contingent which had been formed under the mandate of the 1987 Indo- Sri Lankan accord which aimed to end the civil war being waged between the Sri Lankan forces and the Sri Lankan Tamil nationalists, like the Liberation Tigers of Tamil Eelam (LTTE). With escalation of conflict in the tiny island country, refugees were taking shelter in India. Their main task was to disarm the militant groups and help in restoration of peace by formation of an Interim Administrative Council. The plan had gone well but differences emerged when the LTTE tried to dominate the Council and refused to disarm. He and his comrades had been sent to restore peace in the country and then return to their homeland.

In their many sessions as part of the pre-induction training, the officers of the 35 Bn CRPF explained more about the culture and ethos of the country where they were going to be deployed. They felt that giving a historical perspective to the issue provides a different lens to troops once they are on the ground. This also helps in understanding local sensitivities. Sri Lanka wrested independence from the British in 1948. Turmoil began soon thereafter as the Tamil minority felt discriminated against by the Sinhalese majority. In 1983, civil violence led to the killing of 13 soldiers of the Sri Lankan Army. This was followed by a brutal repression wherein more than 400 Tamils were killed in the 'Black July' riots. Guerrilla warfare followed. June 1987 witnessed large-scale casualties as the Army tried to free Jaffna. They were unsuccessful but it led to a humanitarian crisis. A peace accord was signed on July 29, 1987 and this brought temporary truce.

The first IPKF operation was launched on October 9, 1987. They were to be part of 'Operation Pawan', which was being launched by the Indian Army to exercise control over Jaffna. The task was to neutralise the LTTE's operational capability around Jaffna and capture, or at least control, the LTTE leaders.

The first news coming from Sri Lanka had been encouraging. As expected, the Indian forces had raided and captured the LTTE radio station at Tavadi and their TV station at Kokkuvil. Approximately 200 LTTE soldiers had been captured, but the reverses began thereafter. The LTTE ambushed a CRPF convoy near Tellipallai. Four Jawans made the supreme sacrifice of losing their lives. Another jeep of the 10 Para commandos was ambushed wherein five boys were killed. On the night of 12 October, began the heli-borne assault on Jaffna University, which was the headquarters of the LTTE.

It was a warm October evening when the plane carrying the troops of the CRPF landed in Sri Lanka. Under normal circumstances, Mohanan would have wanted to explore the first foreign country he was visiting but the tension in the air did not permit him to appreciate the scenic beauty. He learnt that the IPKF was making a determined bid to capture Jaffna. The LTTE snipers were known to have taken up positions on rooftops and trees. They were also armed with telescopic infra-red lights and could selectively kill, without wasting any ammunition. They were also targeting the officers and radiomen so as to wipe away the leadership. The roads were mined heavily and convoys were ambushed, taking advantage of the natural terrain which was unfamiliar to the Indians. In addition, the LTTE had mastered the art of guerrilla warfare and merging into the civilian crowds easily. This was compounded by the use of child soldiers.

Jaffna is the capital city of the northern province of Sri Lanka. It is the second most populated city after Colombo. Historically, Jaffna has been a contested city since long with the Portuguese, the Dutch and the British having occupied the city in a long succession of occupations. It is strategically located and hence the struggle for exercising control over it. The majority is Tamilian and therefore sympathetic to the LTTE cause. Mohanan looked around the airport with interest. He had learnt that the Palaly Airport was first built by the Royal Air Force during World War II. Later it came to function as an international airport but during the civil war, it was taken over by the Sri Lankan Air Force. As uniformed crowds milled around, Mohanan realised that they were in the middle of a war.

It was 9.00 a..m on October 15, 1987, when the two CRPF companies started their journey towards Tropo, where they were to relieve 8 Mahar of the Indian Army. The convoy wound its way through the undulating, breathtakingly beautiful terrain. However, Mohanan knew they could not afford to lower their guard. They had been repeatedly briefed to be careful and alert. They had traversed only 6-7 kms when the convoy had to be stopped as a rear vehicle developed a technical snag. The mechanics quickly rectified the defect. However, the snag returned 5 kms later. This time the mechanics were quicker; hence the convoy picked up speed towards its destination.

Just as they took the final turn towards Tropo, gun shots rang out from the hillocks. Suddenly, the air was rent with the sound of automatic gunfire and loud explosions. The troops were caught unawares. There was a moment of shock and then years of training kicked in. Reflexively, their weapons spewed retaliatory fire. The drivers picked up speed in a bid to steer the vehicles out of the ambush area. While the troops with personal weapons fought back, Mohanan knew he had to strike; and strike hard! He was armed with the Light Machine Gun. As the vehicle rolled towards safety, Mohanan let loose the LMG. The automatic weapon gave the necessary fire cover to the driver on move. However, Mohanan was hit by a hail of bullets on the left side of his chest. The left shoulder was hit by a rocket, but Mohanan ensured that his colleagues would retaliate and move to safety. Four personnel of the CRPF and two of the Army were grievously injured in the attack. Mohanan was administered first-aid and air lifted to the hospital. The severe blood loss could not be compensated and the braveheart breathed his last.

After two weeks of bitter fighting, Jaffna was taken over by the Indian forces. The IPKF wrested control of the Tiger's liar by sweeping in through a labyrinth of lanes and bunkers, with concealed alleys and child soldiers lurking in the shadows. The IPKF withdrew from Sri Lanka in March 1990 and the thunder of gunfire was finally stilled in the lush green countryside.

For his conspicuous courage and valour in the face of serious danger, Constable Thankappan Mohanan was posthumously conferred the Vir Chakra. The gallantry award is presented for bravery while facing the enemy in the battle-field. It is the third highest award, after Param Vir Chakra and the Mahavir Chakra.

Today, Mohanan's wife, Padmini, resides in Kollam. Beena, the elder daughter, is an agriculture officer while the younger Nisha has joined the service this year. She was only five months old when Mohanan made the supreme sacrifice at the altar of duty, never having seen her. She gazes at the old photos and has kept every newspaper cutting and scraps that carries the news of her father's bravery and sacrifice. The Vir Chakra occupies a place of pride and reverence in the household.

> *'To every man upon this earth, death cometh soon or late,*
> *And how can man die better,*
> *Than facing fearful odds,*
> *For the ashes of his fathers,*
> *And the temples of his Gods.'*

□

मुहूर्तं ज्वलितं श्रेयो न च धूमायितं चिरम्।।

(महा. उद्योगपर्व—133.15)

One moment of glory is better
than many years of anonymity.

She Kept her Promise

KAMLESH KUMARI

There seemed to be something amiss about the approaching white Ambassador car. Kamlesh stood at Iron Gate No.1 of the Parliament House, which had been witness to hundreds of such cars moving in and out of the gate. But years of training had taught her never to ignore her intuitive feeling. This official-looking Ambassador car had a number of stickers pasted on the windscreen, yet she felt suspicious about it. So she did what had been drilled into her; she moved to alert the others. In the meantime, the car gained entry. Suddenly there was a sound of automatic gunfire. Sensing imminent danger and yet conscious of the gravity of the situation, Kamlesh knew she had to act swiftly. After all, she stood guarding the highest seat of Indian democracy, the Indian Parliament. She was unarmed, but her colleagues had weapons. So she alerted everyone. She, all of a sudden, felt a searing pain which she ignored because the task at hand required immediate action. Her alertness and swiftness ensured that the security personnel acted fast, closing all doors leading to the main building. She took one last glance towards the building that held the hopes and aspirations of millions of her countrymen and then slipped into eternal oblivion.

That day, 13 December 2001, she along with her colleagues at 88 (Mahila) Bn of the Central Reserve Police Force, had boarded the bus from Vikaspuri in west Delhi, where they were temporarily accommodated at the Delhi Armed Police Lines. They had been briefed, yet again, of the importance of their duties and the need to perform with due diligence. She was one of the women deployed for performing frisking and searching vehicles and people at various gates of the Parliament. Today she was to be stationed at Iron Gate No.1. She knew she had been handpicked for these duties by the officers who were very specific about who would beat at the Parliament. Agility, presence of mind, a clean record of service, disciplined, psychologically balanced–these were only some of the attributes that were essential. What was of paramount importance was the ability to withstand long hours of duty diligently and be able to act firmly. All these attributes were collectively to be put to test today.

The highest citadel of democracy was attacked by highly motivated and trained militants who were on a suicide mission. The attack occurred at around 11.40 am when five terrorists, heavily armed in battle fatigues, tried to storm the Indian Parliament which was in session and many of India's political representatives were present in the House. Heavy gunfire ensued in which the security forces confronted the terrorists. The massive doors to the Parliament were closed and as the world watched in amazement, the security forces launched a counter-offensive almost immediately. The

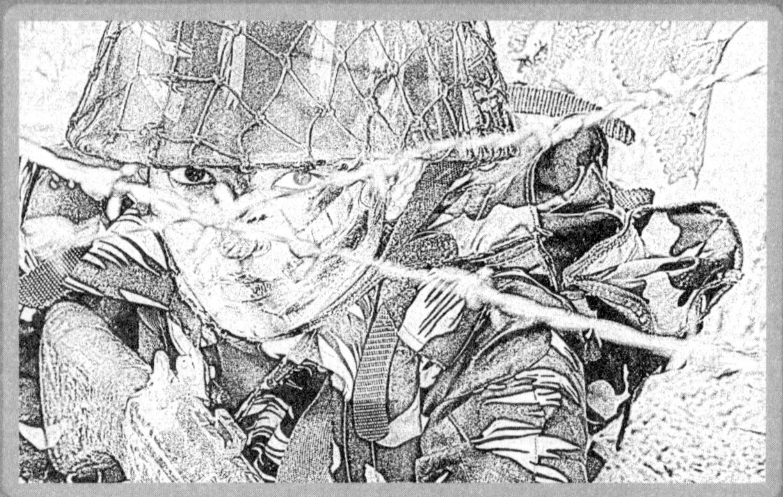

terrorists were gunned down and the sanctity of the citadel was maintained.

Some distance away, Kamlesh's husband, Awdesh Kumar received a phone call from the officers of the battalion asking him to report to the company headquarters immediately. He was really not free for anything. The couple had moved to Delhi recently from Allahabad where Kamlesh was posted with the Rapid Action Force. Delhi had not really suited the family. While the elder daughter, Jyoti had started school in the Kendriya Vidhyalaya, the younger one, Shweta, who was only two year old had been inflicted with some sickness or the other since birth. It was an eye infection these days and a swelling on the leg which had not subsided for about a week. Shweta was cranky today and Awdhesh did not want to leave her with the otherwise kind and helpful neighbours. However, the officer on the other end was insistent. When he said that a Gypsy had been sent for him, Awdesh realised that something was seriously wrong, and terribly wrong at that. He rushed to the waiting Gypsy that had already an officer seated inside, waiting for him. Kamlesh's friend and colleague took little Shweta from her. Lights flashing, the Gypsy weaved its way through Delhi traffic. On the way, a curious Awdesh was told that the Parliament had been attacked by armed militants and Kamlesh had been wounded; that they were on their way to Ram Manohar Lohia Hospital was barely registered. Parliament attacked! He was a mass of raging emotions. He forced himself to remain calm but, not for long. He was outraged at the people who had attacked and outraged at their handlers who could do this. He knew his country was a collection of disparate groups, with hundreds of ethnicities and multiple languages are spoken across the length and breadth of the country. There are religious groups that flourish and yet, being an atheist was not uncommon. The size of the country was amazing and he was aware that many European States were smaller than even Uttar Pradesh. He also knew that his was the second most populous nation in the world and his countrymen differed in caste, race, religion, etc. In fact, in almost every parameter, there were differences. He was often amazed at the fact that there seemed to be so little in common among them, yet he had never met or even heard of anyone who wasn't proud of India's democratic credentials. He could still recall the pride he felt when he'd first seen the majestic building of the Indian Parliament. As he had bowed his head in reverence at the Amar Jawan Jyoti, he had felt he was paying obeisace to every soldier who stood guarding this building. He thought that if there was one icon which could describe India, this must be the one. So when he heard of the attack on the Parliament, he felt as he was kicked in the gut. Someone had the audacity to plan and execute such a sacrilege. He'd fight them himself barehanded, but wouldn't let them reach the hallowed portals of his country's Parliament.

As he sat dumbfounded in the Gypsy, he was so engrossed in his own thoughts that he quite forgot to ask why he was being taken to Ram Manohar Lohia Hospital, one of the biggest hospitals in the city. When the vehicle screeched to a halt, he was amazed to see the number of OB vans and the media persons gathered there. In the confusion that prevailed there, he was whisked away to a secluded place. It was there that it dawned upon him that something had happened. Something was drastically wrong and somehow he was in the middle of it all. They led him to a bed which was shrouded in white. With trembling hands, he uncovered the face. It was someone whom he'd loved all his life and now knew would be proud of today and always. It was Kamlesh, his wife and partner of more than a decade. He removed the white shroud and saw her uniform drenched in blood. This was an image he would never forget all his life. Silently, reverentially, he took a step back, stood erect at attention and saluted the Fallen soldier.

As he sank to his knees, many hands reached out to support him. Dazedly he sat on a chair while someone pushed a glass of water in his hands. He looked up to a harried-looking doctor, who only said, "Eleven bullets; there was nothing we could do..." Awdesh nodded and asked the question that had been troubling him, "The Parliament?" The doctor visibly pulled himself up, "They weren't able to reach inside. We'll get those scoundrels, don't you doubt," and then, may be remembering the gravity of the situation and the loss of this simple soul before him, the doctor patted his shoulder and walked away.

It was in 1987 that Awdesh first saw Kamlesh. He had gone to visit his relatives who stayed in a small town in Uttar Pradesh. As the bus approached Farrukhabad, he had the intuition that life was about to change. Farrukhabad is a bustling town that was founded in 1714 by Nawab Mohammad Khan Bangash, who named it after the reigning Mughal Emperor, Farrukhsiyar. What started as a small place made by a grant of 52 Bamtela villages, was now a township. Awdesh himself belonged to the prosperous city of Kannauj, which is not very far away.

He was unemployed and was resisting the pressure to get married but when he saw her, his opinion changed. Life would be easier with her, he thought. Their first daughter Jyoti was born soon after marriage and life seemed just perfect. He was doing odd jobs and was a skilled tailor.

However, he soon realised that his seemingly delicate wife had dreams–dreams to be different, dreams to do something and achieve the impossible. So when he saw an advertisement in the newspaper calling for applications from young women to join the Central Forces, he took the paper home. And when, after dinner, he showed it to her, her expression said it all. Awdesh was sure this was what Kamlesh wanted to do–an opportunity to wear the uniform, an opportunity to serve the nation and, above all, an opportunity to prove her worth.

So in 1994, she appeared for the selection tests. Days later, the offer of appointment came. The orders said that she had to join at Allahabad and report for training at Neemuch, a small town in Madhya Pradesh. The CRPF was raising the elite Rapid Action Force and Kamlesh was among the first batch of women to so join. Their daughter was only five years old but Awdesh knew his wife's ambition. He was also aware of the needs of the child. So he did the next best thing. He offered to look after the child. Of course, there were difficulties and of course, people questioned his wisdom. Some even went to the extent of ridiculing him for being a house-husband while the wife went out to earn; but, to him, his wife's glowing face was more important. The day she donned the blue camouflaged dungarees of the RAF was as proud a moment for him as for her.

The family moved to Allahabad where Kamlesh was now posted. She often went out on familiarisation exercises in the surrounding areas. Soon she became popular for her polite but firm ways. Awdesh remembered with pride walking with her to the local market in the evenings where everyone seemed to know her. She was also a role model in her native Farrukhabad, where girls would want to emulate her. The family became complete in 2000, when their second daughter, Shweta, was born. A year later they shifted to Delhi on transfer.

A wail brought Awdesh out of his reverie. This was the family of another brave soldier, Nanak Chand, who had made the Supreme Sacrifice at the altar of duty. Awdesh now sought out the details of the incident. Sketchy details emerged. Apparently, five heavily armed militants had tried to storm the Parliament complex. Their nefarious designs had been thwarted by the determined response from the security forces. All five terrorists were killed in the operation that followed. More than a hundred Members of Parliament were inside the building but the alert and prompt action by the security forces ensured that the citadel of democracy was saved.

Awdesh remembered the soul-stirring pledge Kamlesh had taken years ago. At the passing out parade, Kamlesh, along with her colleagues had stood erect and proud. In a solemn ceremony, she had touched the national flag as it went past, held aloft by a special party. The CRPF flag followed. Thereafter came the oath-taking ceremony. Administered by a young officer in Hindi, the words now came back to him...

मैं परमेश्वर को साक्षी मानकर, अपने धर्म से प्रण करती हूँ,
कि हिंदुस्तान और हिंदुस्तान की हुकूमत, जो कानून द्वारा बनाई गई है,
की सच्चे मन से हितैषी रहूँगी और
केंद्रीय रिज़र्व पुलिस बल में अपने धर्म और सच्चाई के साथ सेवा करती रहूँगी।
पवन, जल, भूमि, जिस मार्ग से जाने की आज्ञा होगी, जाऊँगी
और जिसे मेरा अधिकारी स्थापित किया जाएगा, उसकी सारी आज्ञाओं का तन-मन से
पालन करूँगी, चाहे उसमें प्राण जाने का भी भय क्यों न हों।

Kamlesh had lived up to the oath she had taken. She had, in her sacrifice, become an icon of bravery and valour. She had done her family and country proud.

On the Republic Day Parade, 2002, President K.R. Narayan presented the Ashoka Chakra to Kamlesh Kumari posthumously. The Ashoka Chakra is India's highest peace-time military decoration awarded for valour, courageous action or self-sacrifice away from the battlefield. It is the peace-time equivalent of the Param Vir Chakra and is awarded for the "most conspicuous bravery or some daring or pre-eminent valour or self-sacrifice." Today, in their modest home in Kannauj, Awdesh lives with his two daughters. He has but one dream, and that is to fulfil the desires of his late wife. He strives to provide the best possible opportunities to their children. The Ashoka Chakra occupies a place of pride in the house.

He gazes at it ever so often and touches it reverentially–acircular gold gilt. The medal on its obverse has the Ashoka Chakra in the centre, surrounded by a lotus wreath with an ornate edge. It is suspended by a straight-bar suspender. The medal is named on the edge. On the reverse, the word Ashoka Chakra in Hindi appears on the upper edge while along the lower rim, the same is written in English. Awdesh is very proud of his wife and her bravery in the face of imminent danger. Her devotion to duty is a source of inspiration for her colleagues and in her native Farrukhabad, her parents take great pride in being known as Kamlesh's parents. Her in-laws call her 'the brave bahu (daughter-in-law)'. Awdesh says, "We all have to go one day; no one is here forever. The only thing that matters is how you go."

□

को हि भारः समर्थानां किं दूरं व्यवसायिनाम्।
को विदेशः सुविद्यानां कः परः प्रियवादिनाम्।।

Persons possessing power, business acumen, knowledge and courteous behaviour, use these traits to their best advantage for everyone.

Resolute Defender

YAM BAHADUR THAPA

It was December 13, 2001. Head Constable YB Thapa idly saw the day breaking over the horizon, recited his own name–Head Constable Y.B. Thapa and counted the days backwards. It was the 15th day of his having taking over the rank of Head Constable. He savoured the rank name yet again. He was HC Thapa who was now holding charge of Morcha No.1 at the citadel of democracy, the Indian Parliament. He looked at the horizon once more and realised he had half an hour to himself before he had to get dressed. After all, he was now a rank holder and had more time than the constable. He smiled at the thought.

Yam Bahadur Thapa was born and brought up at Shillong. Youngest of the eight siblings, he was the favourite of his parents. He remembered his childhood as tough but enriched with happy times. Originally natives of Nepal, the family had migrated to Shillong years ago and formed part of a tightly-knit community. The family subsisted on cattle and the entire family contributed to their upkeep, often taking the cattle heads grazing. Yam completed his Class VIII from the Madan Laban Nepali Secondary School at Shillong. Never a bright student, he struggled at his classes. The high point in his life was games and the sports activities which ignited a spark in him. Young Yam excelled at all of them. Lying on his bed, he reminisced the day when long ago they had gone up the Shillong Peak on a school excursion. The highest peak overlooking the city mesmerised him. The teacher told them that while there were many myths woven around the legend of the name Shillong, the most popular one held that it derived its name from a young boy, U. Shyllong. About 14 kms south of present-day Shillong, in the village Bissi, resided a young lady called Lir. She gave birth to a stillborn child, whom she named U. Shyllong. The child was dead, so she buried him in her garden. Years later, he appeared at her doorstep at midnight. Assuring her that he recognised her as his mother, he explained that he had come to establish the rule of law and justice. U. Shyllong ('one who grows naturally') is the presiding deity of Shillong. Hearing the story, Yam suddenly understood the reference to the phrase, 'Kot Shillong' or 'Call Shyllong' which the residents still use as a prayer when faced with a danger or in peril, or a misfortune.

On completion of Class VIII, Yam grew into a young lad but lacked direction. He did odd jobs in and around the city. The year was 1985. The country had lost its beloved Prime Minister and there seemed to be turmoil. Then he heard of the Central Reserve Police Force holding an open recruitment drive for the new battalions, which were being raised. He had seen the CRPF Centre at Polo Grounds in Shillong and thus it wasn't intimidating to walk into the recruitment ground of 53 Bn CRPF, which was the recruiting agency. Many of his friends were selected along with him; so, it was with fun and

gaiety that they reported, to the 78 Bn CRPF being raised at Avadi, Madras, as new recruits.

Madras, as it was then called, was a rude shock. Used to the salubrious climate of Shillong, they simply could not adjust to the heat, dust and humidity of the coastal city. From Shillong, known as the Scotland of the east where rolling hills was a common sight and the clouds visited them often, the salty winds of Madras were uncomfortable to say the least. The food was abominable and to someone who had never known sweat or grime, it was a difficult adjustment. The physical exercises seemed very easy to the hill boys, but they seemed fatigued all the time. The entire environs seemed just too much. Every morning they would question themselves whether they should just give up and return home. Each day, one friend or the other counselled the others to hold on. In the end, none of them left. After attestation, he was transferred to 35 Bn CRPF, then located at Jamshedpur. A series of deployments and duties followed wherein he moved across the country with his colleagues and comrades in arms.

On the personal front, in 1988, he married a Nepalese girl, whose family was also settled in Shillong. However, the local conditions deteriorated in the following years and were not conducive to leaving behind a young woman alone. His brother was also in the Army and there was no one to look after the family. The patriarch, who had held the family together for so many years, had passed away. The brothers held a series of consultations among themselves and decided to move the family back to Nepal. Thus, in 1998, very reluctantly, he moved his family to Nepal. India had given him everything. He owed allegiance to the Indian constitution and yet his family no longer felt safe here. He felt the oft-repeated tinge of remorse and squirmed at the thought.

He was brought to the present by the familiar bell of the mess announcing that breakfast was ready and he must make his way to the designated spot. He was deployed at Gate No. 1 of the Indian Parliament. This was the designated gate for the entry of the Union Ministers and the Members of Parliament, along with other dignitaries. The House was in session and hence it was to be a busy day. As in-charge of the sentry post, HC Thapa had a lot to do. At times, it is easier to work yourself than to supervise the work of a fellow human being. He was now responsible for the work and conduct of his juniors. He intended to take his job seriously. He took his assigned carbine from the armoury and walked to the designated place. He closely looked at the weapons of the constables under his command and noted with satisfaction that they gleamed, speaking of good care. His previous posting at 27 Bn Sibsagar had taught him to look at weapons closely. He intended to follow the routine. Never in his dreams could he have visualised that this caution was to save many lives that day.

As the day wore on, many dignitaries came and left. The media was also there in full strength. A House in session meant a lot more work–his superiors had explained earlier and he had watched in fascination as the political leaders of the country gathered here. Suddenly there were a series of loud explosions followed by rapid gunfire. Quick in his reflexes, he ducked and hit the floor. Apparently, some terrorists had entered Gate No. 11 in an official-looking Ambassador car which bore the stickers of many ministries. It also had the national flag on the bonnet and did not stop for the mandatory scrutiny. The wireless sets were shouting instructions and there was commotion due to which very little could be heard. From his vantage position, Thapa saw many persons hit by the indiscriminate firing; some others lay wounded after being hit by the shrapnel of the grenades that were lobbed.

He realised his day of reckoning had come. He now stood between the nefarious designs of the terrorists who had dared to target the highest citadel of democracy–the Indian Parliament. This was not just a building; it was a monument that held the hopes and aspirations of millions of Indians. He was a Nepalese but he had sworn to the document which had been drafted here–the Indian Constitution. He felt a rush of adrenaline in his veins. Calmly, he checked the magazine of his carbine and cocked it. He looked towards his companion, Constable Sukhwinder Singh, who too followed suit. They were ready to take on the terrorists. The first terrorist loomed in front of them. He fired with an automatic rifle and missed them closely. Thapa and Sukhwinder did not give him a second chance. As gunfire erupted, Thapa watched; the bullets found their mark. But the terrorist did not slump as they had expected; rather, he was blown up into smithereens. Sickeningly, he watched the pieces fall next to him. Apparently, the terrorist had worn a suicide belt or jacket which had been accidentally triggered and he was blown away.

However, there was no time to stand and ponder over the possibilities. Gunfire raged around them, interspersed with grenade explosions. The sound was deafening and even as he knew that reinforcements must already be on their way, the onus lay on him to hold on till the officers arrived. He spotted another terrorist moving towards his position, firing in all possible directions. Whatever their plot was, they seemed to be disoriented. He had to take advantage of this. He aimed and fired at this terrorist, who fired back. He saw the look of disbelief in the eyes of the terrorist, who slumped. Simultaneously, he felt a searing pain in his own leg. Apparently, the bullets fired by the terrorist had ricocheted and hit him in the knee. Hot red blood gushed out and pooled. He looked with contempt at the body of the second terrorist and made his way towards the barracks. Dragging his left leg, he made a determined move towards the location. However, the distance proved too long. His exhausted body gave way near the statue of the Father of the Nation, Mahatma Gandhi. As he slumped forward, he thought he saw the apostle of peace and non-violence bless him. Knowing that the Mahatma would approve of his actions, he passed out.

The remaining period passed in the realm between consciousness and semi-consciousness. He was aware of being administered some kind of first-aid but the loss of blood could not be stemmed. The static of gunfire could be heard some distance away but the wireless sets seemed to be screaming. He was aware of the shrill emergent sirens of the ambulance as it whisked him away as he gave one last glance at the majestic Parliament. Oddly, he thought of his young son, who was only three and to whom he had promised to bring sweets. Vaguely he remembered that it was a Thursday and he had looked forward to having rice and *kadhi* for lunch. He remembered the face of his *ustaad* at basic training and who had taught him to fire properly. He was struggling to remember his name when the ambulance came to a screeching halt at Ram Manohar Lohia Hospital. He braced himself to hear the doctors tell him the extent of the injury but before he could do so, he fell into oblivion.

When he came to, there was no pain. He was told two bullets had hit him–one had passed through his calf, but the other was lodged too close to a main artery. Any operation could have risked touching a nerve and it might have led to a permanent disability. Thapa interrupted the well-meaning kind doctor. His own injury was meaningless and held no importance, he insisted. The safety of the Parliament was more important; he wanted to know the details thereof. The solemn doctor broke into a wide grin–all the five terrorists had been eliminated by the brave CRPF personnel. The sanctity of the citadel was intact. Thapa felt the tension leave his body; all else was well! He would heal.

He remained in the hospital for a fortnight and was discharged with clear instructions of not putting any pressure on the leg. The media feted him and he was acclaimed a hero. Ministers and dignitaries visited him in the hospital and he was exalted for his bravery. However, all he wanted to do was to meet his family. Communication was poor to the village where his wife lived and there was little point in alarming her. The children were young too. She had come to know, of course. The erratic radio communication had carried the news to her but it was sketchy at best. She knew that the terror attack on the Indian Parliament had been foiled but did not know of his role in it. She did not know he was injured and he had preferred not to tell her either. Once he had healed sufficiently, he requested for leave which was immediately granted. He flew to Nepal on New Year's eve.

It was an overnight journey to his village from Kathmandu. It was biting cold and his leg throbbed mercilessly, It became numb as the bus traversed the hilly terrain on a rough road. He reached at noon, just as the sun warmed up and circulation returned to his leg. The family was overjoyed to see him. His wife watched his gait warily, but he smiled. Before he could get the opportunity to tell her, the local priest came calling. Thapa was chided for having missed the community worship of the *'Kuldevi'*. This had not gone down well in the community and would surely bring bad luck in the coming years. The wife was listening to her husband being chastised, looking downcast and ashamed. Thapa listened patiently, as the priest went on about ill omens. The neighbours had gathered and it wasn't a pretty sight. Thapa's elder brother, who was in the Indian Army and on leave too, suddenly stopped the priest mid-sentence. This was unprecedented. He then went on to provide a detailed account of what had happened on that fateful day in Delhi and the role of the younger Thapa in neutralising the attack. He spoke eloquently and with obvious pride. The younger Thapa then showed the marks of the gruesome injury and the newspaper clippings he had carried with him. From the corner of his eye, he saw his wife's face cloud with horror and concern. Then he saw the pride and dignity of an honour restored.

HC Thapa was awarded the Shaurya Chakra for his valour and courageous action. In the face of imminent danger, Thapa did not flinch. His bravery and fearlessness had saved the day. At the Defence Investiture ceremony, the President, Dr. APJ Abul Kalam pinned the medal on his proud chest. As Thapa walked back, he knew he had made his tryst with destiny and emerged victorious.

□

योग न राष्ट्र स्निह्यति, न स स्नेहं क जानीते।

He who loves not his country can love nothing.

Unflinching Courage

D. SANTOSH KUMAR

Santosh looked up at the majestic building and felt a deep sense of pride. He was gazing at the citadel of democracy–the Indian Parliament. This was the building that held the hopes and aspirations of millions of Indians across the country. As a proud soldier of 23 Bn Central Reserve Police Force, he stood admiring the building which guarded the rights of his countrymen. Looking up at the majestic portals of the Parliament, he remembered a stirring moment which was still fresh in his mind.

Just six months ago, he had completed his basic training with the CRPF. On the Attestation Day, he had sworn allegiance to the Indian Constitution. The pledge meant everything to him. He smiled as he thought of the Recruit Training Centre, Neemuch and his association with it.

A native of Ghazipur in Uttar Pradesh, Santosh was brought up in Hyderabad. His father served in the Central Reserve Police Force and the family moved to the CRPF campus. The family opted to behind in order to provide better education to the children. Santosh, along with his siblings which included an elder sister and a younger brother, was enrolled in the Kendriya Vidhyalaya, CRPF, Hyderabad. He was good at his studies and it was an exposure to the Scouts and Guides which helped to seal his choice of a career. Growing up in a CRPF campus, he was impressed with the Force and felt a deep bond with the Force. When there was a recruitment rally in the campus, he applied and was selected. There was never a shadow of doubt. He was asked to report to RTC at Neemuch.

Neemuch is a small town in the Malwa region of Madhya Pradesh. It holds the distinction of being the birthplace of the CRPF and hence a highly revered place. Originally a large British Cantonment, it had become the seat of the Rajptana Malwa political agency. In 1939, the Crown Representative's Police Force was raised here. After Independence, the Iron man of India, Sadar Vallabh Bhai Patel had argued for the necessity of such a Force in the federal structure of the new Nation. Thus, the Force was retained and renamed as the Central Reserve Police Force.

Santosh had heard of the city and the tales of bravery shown by the CRPF; yet, nothing had prepared him for the majesty and aura of Neemuch. The place throbbed with CRPF officers who were its life and blood. As he entered the hallowed portals of the Victoria Barracks, it seemed that the place whispered tales of glory of the generations gone by. The next day when he reported at the grounds, wearing a crisp new uniform, he could feel the toil and hard work of the hundreds who must have been trained here. Painted in bold letters was a sign which read–'The more you sweat in training, the less you bleed in war'. A shiver went up his spine.

He vowed to take his training very seriously.

When the time came for the Passing Out Parade, all his friends joined in the celebrations. Santosh, however, felt a deep sense of loss as his father's absence as the latter had dreamt of witnessing his son take the oath on the Attestation Day parade. The patriarch had passed away suddenly. This was a bolt from the blue. His father had risen to the rank of a Head Constable. Santosh missed his father acutely on this special day; it was not easy to hold back his tears.

It is a regular practice to send trained recruits to operational units to induct youngsters, but he was in for a surprise. While all the new personnel were allotted field postings, he was sent to a Unit in Delhi. This too was marked with poignancy for him as he was alloted to 23 Bn CRPF, which was his father's unit. He accepted this as a blessing from his father and promised to follow in his father's footsteps.

The short but subdued alarm from his watch told him that it was time for his duty at the Parliament House. Routinely, personnel work in shifts of two hours each. This is to ensure alertness at all times. His allotted turn was in the 1100 hrs to 1300 hrs shift. Santosh was on duty at Gate No.11 which was very close to Gate No. 1–the designated gate for entry of VIPs.

The morning wore on as vehicles one after another whizzed past the imposing gates. The usual media crowd too was in full attendance. The House had adjourned for the day but many people were still inside the precincts of the building. A few hangers-on soaked in the mild warmth of the winter sun. Santosh looked around at these important people and idly wondered what could be going on in their minds as they walked past.

Suddenly a loud explosion shook him from his reverie. This explosion was followed by a milder one. Fresh from training, he immediately recognised the sound of gunfire. He was taken aback as he had not expected to hear this sound in the heart of Delhi, let alone the Parliament House. His senses on high alert, he looked towards his commander. In a silent communication, they got into action, readying their firearms to face the unexpected. Concurrently, they moved to occupy vantage positions. From his position behind a tree, Santosh cautiously peered at the wide vista that lay in front of him. Four people loomed in front of his eyes. Heavily armed, four strangers stood, firing indiscriminately. It was clear that they were looking for an entry into the building. His worst fears were confirmed as he realised that the Parliament House was under armed attack.

Taking an aimed shot, the Ustad's words at the training camp rang in his mind. He took a deep breath and fired. The bullet went flying past and he saw a terrorist slump to the ground. There was very little time to feel anything much. The second terrorist was also brought down in the same manner. The self-loading rifle was firing on an automatic mode and soon the magazine ran empty. Calmly, with months of rigorous training behind him, Santosh changed the magazine without even looking down. His eyes never left the enemy. However, by this time, the remaining two terrorists had spotted him and turned to fire at him. Santosh was a tad swifter than them. The bullet hit one terrorist in the abdomen. With an incredulous look in his eyes, he slumped. The remaining terrorist made a mad rush to escape from Santosh's weapon by turning round a corner. In the far distance, shots of gunfire could be heard. He knew that his colleagues must be battling with the lone remaining terrorist.

Minutes later, he came to know that the last terrorist had been gunned down. Santosh touched the warm barrel of his rifle; it had saved the day. It was only appropriate that training received at the birthplace of the CRPF had been put to test at the biggest challenge a CRPF personnel could face. The CRPF emerged victorious and his father's teachings had helped him in achieving his aim of steadfastly performing a duty without flinching.

The Shaurya Chakra is awarded for conspicuous bravery and valour in the face of adversity. The medal was conferred on Santosh at a solemn Defence Investiture Ceremony at the Ashoka Hall of Rashtrapati Bhavan. Santosh was feted by the media and the public alike. Years later, he visited the Parliament House with his wife Sindhu and daughter Saumya. He admired the hallowed portals which have remained unscathed. Today, he is a proud soldier who has ensured that the CRPF has lived up to its motto, 'Service and Loyalty'.

□

यावद्बद्धो मरुद देहे यावच्चित्तं निराकुलम्।
यावद्दृष्टिभ्रुवोर्मध्ये तावत्कालभयं कुतः ॥

So long as the breath is restrained in the body,
so long as the mind is undisturbed,
and so long as the gaze is fixed,
there is no fear from Death.

Unwavering Resolve

SUKHWINDER SINGH

December 13, 2001. Sukhwinder Singh of the 23 Bn Central Reserve Police Force walked to his designated sentry post at Gate No. 1 of Parliament House. The House was in session and he knew this was important. He had been with 23 Bn CRPF since 1992. His long association with this unit meant he knew almost each one of his colleagues. His commander, Head Constable Y.B. Thapa had reported to the Unit just 15 days ago. The Parliament House is a huge complex; it is also a busy place, especially when it is in session.

Sukhwinder was on a two-hour shift duty from 11.00 hrs. He wanted to take his place at the sentry post before the appointed time. He quickly wore his bullet-proof jacket and picked up his SLR. As he walked towards the post, he realised that discipline came naturally to him. When he was barely 10-years old, his father had sought voluntary retirement from the Army and returned to the family home at Ghot Pokhar in Gurdaspur, Punjab. His father had drilled discipline in his children. After his mother passed away, young Sukhwinder devoted his time to studying at the local Government Senior Secondary School.

Ghot Pokhar is a small town on the outskirts of Gurdaspur. Located in the fertile area between the Beas and Ravi rivers, the town's history is moulded by its geography. Founded by Mahant Guriyaji at the beginning of the 17th century, the town was a flashpoint during India's Independence. At the stroke of the midnight hour, when India awoke to freedom, Gurdaspur was still unsure of its status. The communal fabric of the country was frayed, and more so in Gurdaspur. The Boundary Award had not been declared and people did not know whether to celebrate or otherwise. The area was predominantly inhabited by Muslims but if the natural boundary line of Ravi river were to be followed, the district would go to India. The dawn of August 17 brought the news of the location of the line, which was to draw a permanent wedge between the neighbours. The Radcliffe Award gave Shakargarh to Pakistan and the rest remained with India. Mass migrations followed. Partition was to leave a permanent scar on the Gurdaspur psyche. Gurdaspur Darbar Sahib at Kartarpur which houses the famous Sikh temple, where Guru Nanak Dev spent his last days, was awarded to Pakistan. In the turmoil that followed, people did not realise the enormity of what was to follow in the years to come. Gurdaspur was to become one of the quirks of Fate that was to shape the history of the subcontinent in the years to come.

The new neighbours were soon locked in a mortal duel over the snowy mountains. With the fate of Kashmir uncertain, Pakistan backed the attack by Kabailis on Kashmir in October 1947. The Indian Army responded to the crisis by sending men and equipment through the only land route to Kashmir that lay

through Gurdaspur. Unwillingly, the people of this small town got involved. The conflict was to leave a permanent mark on the people and is reflected in the folklore and stories woven around the events.

The eighties also witnessed turbulent times for the city. Punjab went through an extreme form of militancy. Gurdaspur was deeply affected, more so because of its strategic location. The highly patriotic people of this region responded by joining the Armed Forces in large numbers. Sukhwinder's elder brother joined the Army. When CRPF carried out the open recruitment drive at Police Lines, Gurdaspur, it was only natural for Sukhwinder to join. A few days later, he was on his way to the Group Centre at Pinjore for equipping and then on to Gauhati where 105 Bn CRPF was being raised. A year later, he was transferred to the 23 Bn CRPF. A series of deployments and postings followed. By 2001, he had spent a long tenure in the same Unit. A strong sense of regimentation ensured that he knew most people of the unit. He was brought back to the present by the sounds around him. The Unit had truly become his second home. He nodded at the personnel as he made his way to the sentry post. Head Constable Y.B. Thapa was already present there.

The first half hour passed swiftly. It was a busy day for the Parliament and many vehicles whizzed in and out of Gate No. 1, where he was deployed. It was around 11.40 am when he saw a rather agitated female constable run towards them. Sensing something amiss, Sukhwinder became alert. The unmistakable sound of gunfire followed a loud explosion. Reflexively, Sukhwinder raised his SLR and was ready to take on the adversary. He also moved to take position behind a wide tree which could afford greater protection.

Sure enough, a militant loomed into clear view. He was

firing indiscriminately as he moved towards the steps leading to the main building of Parliament House. As bullets whizzed past the duo, they fired back. Suddenly, his body was thrown up into the air and fell into pieces. Apparently, he had strapped explosives on his body which had blown him apart. However, the immediate threat had been thwarted.

As he lowered his weapon and turned away from the sight, Shukhwinder felt a searing pain in his stomach. He looked at the ground and saw it turn red as blood gushed out from his abdomen, forming a pool of blood around him. Disbelievingly, he looked at his colleague, Head Constable Thapa, who was clutching his knee and seemed to be in agony. Sukhwinder quickly assessed that both of them had been injured and needed immediate medical aid. He remembered his first-aid classes wherein he had learnt that the adrenaline rush masks the initial pain in the injury.

Wireless systems crackled. The duo radioed the news. Reinforcements rushed to them and took over the post. Clutching each other, the duo made their way to the barracks. They managed to reach some distance before collapsing into the arms of their colleagues, who rushed them to Ram Manohar Lohia Hospital.

The ambulance wove its way across the streets of Delhi. Sukhwinder slipped in and out of consciousness. Once he was sure that the terrorists had been eliminated and the political leaders were all safe, Sukhwinder slipped into deep sleep. Thinking of his two-year old daughter, he consoled himself that he would recover. A successful operation followed during which, the bullets were extracted. He learnt that his bullet-proof jacket had saved his life. His vital organs had not been damaged. He remained in ICU for the next two days, but held on to the memories of his son, who was only four-years old.

The medical officers announced him out of danger three days later. His brother regaled him with stories of his heroism and courage. When he was discharged from the hospital some 15 days later, he made a special request. He wanted to gaze at the Parliament House one more time. He remembers the special feel of overwhelming reverence he had felt that day as he gazed long at the majestic building that houses the collective will of the millions of his countrymen. The brick and mortar of the Parliament represent the emotions and feelings of the teeming Indians who have placed their faith there. As its custodian, he had lived upto the pledge he had taken and reposed faith in the country his ancestors had chosen decades ago.

Sukhwinder Singh was awarded the Shaurya Chakra for his unflinching courage and bravery in face of imminent danger. He is a role model for many in his town. Posted to Group Centre at Hiranagar, near Jammu, Sukhwinder is modest about his gallantry. "I did what any CRPF person would have done," he shrugs.

□

शक्तिः दुर्दम्येच्छाशक्त्या आगच्छति।

Strength comes from an indomitable will.

Firm Resolve

SHYAMBIR SINGH

It was a winter morning as Shyambir walked towards the sentry post at Gate No. 5 of Parliament House. Winters in Delhi have a chill. This day was no different. The warmth of the sun was comforting. The Parliament was in session and it was to be a busy day. Shyambir was deployed with the Special Duty Group of the Central Reserve Police Force. This is a specialised wing of the CRPF, which is deployed for the protection of the Prime Minister's residence. With the Parliament in session, the Prime Minister was slated to visit and therefore, a small component of the SDG had to be present at the Parliament. The designated gate for the entry of the Prime Minister's carcade was Gate No. 5.

It was 11.00 am by the time Shyambir walked towards the gate to occupy his position. He had been on duty for two consecutive days. Now it was supposed to be a day of rest for him. However, the officers had assured that he would be granted an off day the next day. Shyambir had looked forward to a day of rest. He had planned to proceed on leave later that month and wanted to use the time to buy some gifts for his youngest daughter. He smiled as he thought of her.

Nagariya is a small village, approximately 40 kms away from Mathura in Uttar Pradesh; a small village of less than a hundred families. It is a closely-knit community which functions like an extended family. Shyambir's father was a farmer. Hard work was simply a way of life. His father's elder brother was employed with the Central Reserve Police Force at Srinagar. He had often asked Shyambir to enrol but the father had always refused permission. CRPF was a tough job and he did not want his only son to be away. When Shyambir's sister moved to London to join her husband, his father became more possessive about him. It was in the face of massive opposition at home that he decided to enrol with the CRPF. In an open recruitment drive at Pinjore, Shyambir was selected. When the time came to join at CRPF Training Centre at Pallipuram in Kerala, Shyambir's family stepped up the opposition. With the quiet support of his wife, he joined. Pallipuram came as a shock. It was nowhere close to the life he had experienced till now. The weather, food, ambience, culture, language– nothing was same as at home. He was homesick and missed his friends and family. To make up, he made a conscious effort to seek friendship with people of his own region. Since there was no one from his own belt, he struck up conversations with people from Jhunjhunu and other parts of Rajasthan. It wasn't the same but he managed. However, once the training began, days passed in a blur. Language and regions stopped to matter as he realised that strong bonding develops when people perform together as a team.

After attestation, he was posted to 86 Bn CRPF. The deployments and service took him to Nagaland and then to

Srinagar. The diversity of the country never ceased to amaze him. He became very proud of the CRPF which respects each region and culture. When nominations were sought for transfer to the elite Special Duty Group of the CRPF, he volunteered. He cleared the special tests and psychological assessments easily and was put through intensive training for three months.

Now he had been with the SDG since 1996 and knew the Parliament complex well. Shyambir walked towards his post, thinking of the India-Pakistan cricket match being played and the fact that he would miss it. The Parliament session started in time but was soon adjourned. Many politicians left. He remained alert as Gate No.5 was used for departure by the dignitaries. Suddenly the lull was broken by the sound of crackers. This was unusual. Still unable to comprehend the source of the sound, nonetheless, Shyambir readied himself to meet any eventuality.

There was a huge explosion. The wireless sets crackled. His worst fears were confirmed. The unthinkable was unfolding in front of him. The highest citadel of democracy, the Indian Parliament was under attack. Suddenly, a terrorist appeared in his line of sight. He carried a heavy backpack and was firing indiscriminately. Shyambir knew what had to be done. Calmly, he moved the safety catch of his rifle from 'Safe' to 'Ready'. Never once did he lose sight of the terrorist who was approaching the post. As soon as the terrorist stepped inside the porch of the building next to Gate No. 5, Shyambir swerved around the pillar and opened fire. He did not miss; the terrorist slumped to the ground.

An hour later, the firing stopped. Reinforcements had rushed in much earlier. However, it was imperative that the ground be cleared. The area was combed by the special Forces before an all-clear signal was sounded. Shyambir had already learnt that all the five terrorists had been killed before they could step into the hallowed portals of the Parliament House. In the bloodbath, many of his colleagues had been injured while others had made the supreme sacrifice at the altar of duty. However, it was a matter of satisfaction and pride that the CRPF had ensured that no harm came upon the parliamentarians.

He was feted for his courage and bravery. The media surrounded him and the politicians spoke warmly about the CRPF which had saved the day. An out-of -turn promotion was announced. All along, Shyambir wanted to meet his family. His village had poor connectivity and his house did not have a telephone. The owner of the lone telephone in the village, obliged, by calling his father over the line. Shyambir was able to hear the pride and satisfaction in the voice of his father as it crackled over the wires. Suffused with emotion, he blessed the son whom he loved and hence wanted to protect. The son's actions had protected democracy.

Shyambir was conferred the Shaurya Chakra which is awarded for unusual bravery and gallantry in the face of imminent threat. At the glittering award ceremony held at the Ashoka Hall of the Rashtrapati Bhavan, Shyambir was accompanied by his father and elder son. The three generations held hands on the grounds and as they peered over the imposing Parliament building, they vowed to protect all that it stood for.

□

स्वस्मै स्वल्पं समाजाय सर्वस्वं।

A little bit for Yourself and
Everything for Others!

Unflinching Courage

VIZOTO TINYI

Vizoto Tinyi, a young Naga officer, looked around at the splendour of the Ashoka Hall at Rashtrapati Bhavan as he sat on his designated chair, feeling a deep sense of awe and admiration at the ornately decorated hall. It seemed to take on a special aura for the Defence Investiture Ceremony. Vizoto Tinyi, Assistant Commandant, CRPF was invited to receive the Shaurya Chakra.

A hush descended on the Ashoka Hall. The President, Dr. A.P.J. Abdul Kalam arrived as the National Anthem was being played. The solemn investiture ceremony began. Vizoto sat attentively, hearing the tales of bravery and courage being read out. And then, he heard in crisp tones- Shri Vizoto Tinyi, Assistant Commandant, CRPF, Shaurya Chakra. Smartly he walked to the designated place. Citation for his bravery shown on July 5, 2005 was read out. He marched to the Supreme Commander of the Armed Forces, the President of India, who conferred the Shaurya Chakra on the young officer. The hall erupted in applause. Vizoto marched back to his seat. The Shaurya Chakra is circular in shape and made of bronze. It is one and three-eighth inches in diameter, with rims on both sides. On the obverse of the medal is embossed a replica of Ashoka's chakra in the centre, surrounded by a lotus wreath. Along the rim, the inner side displays a pattern of lotus leaves, flowers and buds. On its reverse, the words SHAURYA CHAKRA are embossed, both in Hindi and English, with the two versions separated by two lotus flowers.

Once back to his designated seat, Vizoto recalled the incident which had brought him to the Ashoka Hall. As a young officer, he joined the 33 Battalion of the CRPF in 2005. The Unit headquarters were based in the bustling city of Faizabad. One company was deployed within the red zone of the disputed site at Ayodhya. A careful and conscientious officer, Tinyi found out all the details and legends associated with the town.

Ayodhya, also known as Saketa, is a small town adjacent to Faizabad in Uttar Pradesh. It is an ancient city and is believed to be the birthplace of Rama and the capital of the Kosala kingdom. Today, it is considered as one of the seven most important pilgrimage sites or *saptapuri* for the Hindus. The Sanskrit word *yudh* means a 'fight' or 'wage a war'. The word 'Ayodhya' thus means 'not to be fought' or 'invincible'. The *Atharvaveda* refers to it as the 'invincible city of the gods' and is a mythical city of gods with eight circles and nine entrances. The *Adi Purana* states that the city 'does not exist by its name, but by its merit'. It also mentions that Ayodhya is called Saketa because of its magnificent buildings which had significant banners as their arms. A different interpretation is by *Satyopakhyana* which states that Ayodhya actually means 'that which cannot be conquered by sins'. Legend has it that

the city was established by Manu, the progenitor of mankind and one who gave it to Ikshvaku to rule.

Vizoto remembered the famous story of Lord Rama he had heard many times. Valmiki's *Ramayana* is an epic on the life and times of Rama, who is said to belong to the city of Ayodhya, the capital of Kosala. Broadly, the story narrates that King Dashrath of Ayodhya had four sons. Rama, his eldest son was exiled for fourteen years. While he was in the forest with his wife Sita and younger brother Lakshman, Sita was kidnapped by the demon-king Ravana and taken to Sri Lanka. A fierce battle ensued between Rama and Ravana, in which the latter was killed. Rama returned to Ayodhya and became the king of Ayodhya. He established the 'Ramrajya' which became the ideal kingdom. Ramayana and its characters find mention in folklore and many festivals are celebrated around the tale. The most important festival of the Hindus, Diwali, which is celebrated to mark the return of Rama to Ayodhya on return from exile. It marks the triumph of Good over Evil and is popular as the festival of lights. As Vizoto prepared to visit the city which appears commonly in Indian folklore, he found that the legend had many variations. It is scripted differently in different cultures and places. In fact, the cities of Ayutthaya and Yogyakarta in Thailand and Indonesia respectively, are also named after Ayodhya. The city is also holy to the Jains who believe that five Tirthankaras were born here.

The Ramjanmabhoomi-Babri Masjid dispute had led to the deployment of the Central Reserve Police Force at Ayodhya. The issue was sensitive as it had the capability of acquiring communal overtones. In his training, he had been briefed repeatedly on how passions can flare on such occasions.

As he explored the small town, Vizoto found that Ayodhya was a nondescript, dusty town with numerous lanes and bylanes dotted with temples and shrines, all bearing some relation to the story of *Ramayana*. The Hanumangarhi temple or Hanuman's fort situated here is four-sided with circular bastions at each corner and is the most popular temple. Seventy-six steps lead up to a massive place which is believed to have been a cave, from where Hanuman guarded Ayodhya. Vizoto's commanders had told him that this place was held in reverence by thousands. However, it was also a sensitive place where passions could flare. The issue was sub-judice and, as an officer on duty, Vizoto had to maintain the highest standards of impartiality. His job was to uphold the supremacy of law at all times. It was under these circumstances that Vizoto took over the command of the company. The disputed site was a sensitive location and its importance could not be undermined.

Vizoto remembered July 7, 2005 as any other day. The *darshan* started under the strict vigilance of the State police and the CRPF. As usual, a throng of devotees waiting patiently. Vizoto, as company commander of D/33 Bn, was on duty inside the Isolation Zone when he heard the sound of a loud blast, followed by gunfire. It was 9.15 am and he knew there would be chaos. For a second, he was stunned and then years of training kicked in. He acted on reflex grip to the crux of the issue.

As he moved towards the sound of the explosion, he quickly reviewed the security cordons, sentry posts, their positions and his own position. He knew the CRPF was well equipped to deal with any catastrophe, but it was his job as a commander to provide guidance and leadership. Between rapid gunfire and lobbing of grenades, he crawled towards a tactical position. Shouting instructions to the bewildered crowds, he instructed them to lie low as the bullets whizzed past. He quickly assessed that the outer cordon had been breached and the terrorists were trying to enter the Red Zone through the Sita Rasoi. Crawling, he made his way towards Morcha No. 1, occupied by Constables Ram Prasad, Rajesh Kumar and Jaswinder Singh. By assessing the direction and volley of the gunfire, Vizoto inferred that two terrorists were trying to enter, while a third was providing them covering gunfire. This was thwarted by the CRPF men who had taken up strategic positions. By now, Vizoto had reached Morcha No 2. The terrorists were firing indiscriminately at this morcha. The Jawans were retaliating. Just as Vizoto and Inspector Nand Kishore were chalking out a strategy, a stray bullet hit the inspector. Blood gushed out. As he fell to the ground, Vizoto turned to swiftly bandag the oozing wound and then returned to retaliating the onslaught by the terrorists. As the gunfight raged, one more Jawan got grievously injured. Under the hail of bullets, Vizoto undertook the dangerous mission of moving the injured to safety. Once he was able to successfully pull out the injured, he renewed his efforts to neutralise the attack by the terrorists. The wireless systems crackled as instructions were shouted and reinforcements rushed in. Within the Isolation Zone, Vizoto presumed that while the party attacking Morcha 2 had been neutralised, gunshots could still be heard at Morcha 2A.

Without a second thought, Vizoto started the long crawl in open ground towards the *morcha* where his men were retaliating, while looking for their commander's guidance and direction. Vizoto knew this was a perilous mission and fraught with danger. Bullets whizzed past and grenades were lobbed at him, but he continued with his slow crawl. The others tried to provide covering fire. Vizoto managed to reach the relative safety of the *morcha*. With his acumen combined with the presence of their commander, the troops were able to retaliate and effectively hold ground. Soon the gunfire stopped as all the five terrorists were shot down. The sanctity of the site was preserved.

The CRPF's presence of mind, devotion to duty and unflinching courage in the face of eminent danger had saved the day. It was later revealed that the terrorists, owing allegiance to the Lashkar-e-Toiba, had entered India through Nepal. The five terrorists were able to break into the security cordon after securing a jeep. Hurling grenades and firing indiscriminately, they had tried to breach the inner cordon but were successfully thwarted. A civilian, who happened to be near the blast site, died on the spot.

His dexterity and bravery in the face of danger ensured that all five militants were killed. No devotee was harmed and the brave CRPF men ensured that the inner cordon was not breached. The country was saved from an imminent communal carnage.

As he reminisced on this day etched vividly in his memory, Vizoto looked at his younger brother, a pastor, who was accompanying him to this investiture ceremony. He quietly mused about the journey which had brought him here from the hills of Nagaland. Born in a farmer's family residing in a remote village of Kikriima in the Pfutsero Circle of Phek district in Nagaland, he was the fourth sibling in a family of six children. He could vividly remember his happy childhood despite confronting constant struggle. It is a small village with less than 1,500 families knit into clans. His father, Shri H. Tinyi had studied up to Class 4 and his mother did not know the alphabets. But, they were determined to send their children to school and provide them a decent education. The siblings were thus sent to the local village school where

Vizoto studied up to Class 3. In 1984, the family took the momentous decision to shift to Dimapur, the financial hub of Nagaland. Here, their life changed forever. At the Christian English School in Dimapur, Vizoto learnt of life beyond the confines of his village and was filled with wonder. Every day was marked with a new exposure and he could not have enough. His evenings were filled with regaling his parents with all that he had learnt at school.

It was on one such evening when he was recounting his experiences of the new world, he remarked that they could now forget Kikriima. He could never forget the expression on his father's face at the casual comment. His father was pained at the comment and walked away. That night, the siblings were all called to gather. The father said he felt it was time to renew their connection to their roots. The parents narrated the fascinating story of their rich heritage and the battle of Kikriima.

In the aftermath of various battles, which were fought between 1824-26, the British occupied Assam and Manipur. The Naga Hills were known for their inaccessibility. Remote, undulating land with steep slopes and thick forests made the area secluded. The Nagas were also known as staunchly fierce and independent tribe who valued their independence. The lure of tea plantations had brought the British to these lands. Large tracts of land were taken over for plantations. The Nagas responded with raids and killing of the planters. The colonial officers retaliated and the first expedition took place in 1832 with more than 700 soldiers and 800 coolies. This was met with fierce resistance by the Angami Nagas, who rolled stones and used spears to stall the attack. The British, led by Major Butler, tried negotiations for subduing them, but it never worked with the proud Nagas. Fierce battles and violence ensued. However, in face of the British weaponry, the Nagas never really had a chance. The 'hostile villages' were plundered, granaries were put to fire and valuables were confiscated. Yet the Nagas continued to fight relentlessly. A particular village that put up a stiff resistance was Khonoma. After being unsuccessful at numerous atempts, the British sent reinforcements and better weaponry for the expedition. A particularly fierce encounter followed. Shelling continued till the Naga warriors accepted that their spears were futile against the superior arms and fled into the hills. Khonoma had fallen and Major Butler retired to the plains. He wrote, "I do not recommend violent measures, unless we are opposed. We have driven the enemy from his stronghold and it is a question to be considered whether it would not be more advisable not to interfere with the internal matters of the Nagahs."

Against this backdrop, the British troops awaited orders from the headquarters. On February 5, 1851, Captain Reed found that two heralds from Kikriima had come to seek his audience. Intrigued, he met them and to his disquiet, they presented him with a magnificent spear and conveyed an open challenge by Kikriima village to the British government.

Captain Reed was dumbfounded. Here were two people, in the middle of a jungle, conveying a challenge to His Royal Majesty. Addressing Captain Reed, they invited him "to come and prove who had the greatest power in these hills–they [Kikrüma] or our government." The messengers added that, "the Manipuris from Imphal Valley were afraid to fight them and now the British seemed afraid also." They added, "Your *sipahees* are flesh and blood as well as we and we will fight with spear and shield, and see who are the best men."

Now Captain Reed had no option but to accept and "uphold

the name and honour of the government by accepting the challenge." He knew that the village had around 1,000 families and the warriors were known to be determined, daring and fierce. Following the characteristic policy of 'divide and rule', Reed got 800 'friendly Nagahs' to fight against the Kikriimas. Instead of approaching the village from the heavily fortified south as expected, he launched the attack from the poorly-defended north.

It was February when the annual festival of Sukrunyi had been celebrated and preparations were underway to concentrate on the agricultural cycle. The Nagas had cut and cleared the hills painstakingly. The slopes were steep and preparation of the paddy fields was no mean task. The *riiza*, a unique rain-water harvesting system of the Chakhesang tribe, had been checked and the families were ready. They now awaited the declaration of the auspicious day, by the village Thiivo-o, the village priest, for sowing the first seeds.

On February 11, 1851, the British began the ascent at daybreak. Soon, rifles were fired at the village. In face-to-face encounters, the Kikriimas were invincible. However, their spears and shields provided little defence against the raining bullets. The 1st and 2nd Assam Light Infantry killed or wounded most of them. In the consternation that followed, there was utter chaos. The 'friendly Nagahs' wrecked the village, setting their granaries on fire. With fascinated children hanging on to each word, the father continued with his story. This was a tale every head of the family had told his children. This was their heritage and their past. The father spoke with great pain as he reeled off the names of the long-slained ancestors. Vivid pictures flashed in the mind of young Vizoto, as he imagined the proud warriors falling to British bullets. The father's voice continued with the tale.

When day fell, there were only six houses left in the smoldering ashes of the village. When the troops withdrew, they found the elderly, children and women near the west gate. A massacre followed. The British archives describe it as follows: "Thus fell Kekre-mah, after one of the most bloody battles fought in Assam".

As he sat in the Rashtrapati Bhavan, Vizoto could not help but remember his ancestors who, more than 160 years ago, had the daring and determination to challenge the British Empire. It had cost them dearly though it was a remarkable act of resistance and courage. It was also an act of bravery of a single village taking on the might of an empire. An act which resonates with the community even today! His father wanted the children to learn about their past and never ever forget their roots. Vizoto looked at his brother and knew a similar thought would have passed through his mind. He was sure their father was now looking at him, blessing him from Heaven.

His mind again went back to Dimapur and his journey to reach here. He recalled the day of his graduation from Patkai Christian College, Dimapur. Delhi beckoned. Vizoto knew his family's financial background did not permit much. Along with two other friends from a similar background, he left for Delhi on the assurance of a distant cousin. This did not turn out well as they had not applied for admission to Delhi University on provisional certificates. Therefore they could not manage to get admission to any college. A blank wasted year loomed ahead. Since returning to Nagaland was not a feasible option, they decided to prepare for other competitive exams while simultaneously pursuing post-graduation in political science. Time flew thereafter. One friend joined the Army, another returned to Nagaland to join as a lecturer while the third was selected in the State Civil Service examination. Vizoto had heard of the CPO's exam from Shri E. Epao, the first Naga CRPF officer. Vizoto set his eyes on this exam and applied for it in 2000. He was selected in 2001 and reported at the CRPF Academy in November 2001.

A punishing training schedule followed. The days were filled with activity and the mind was challenged to study new subjects. Vizoto soon finished the numerous training sessions. He then reported for his first field posting to Faizabad, a small town in Uttar Pradesh, which had caught the imagination of the entire nation. Destiny had brought this young man from the remote Naga Hills to this small town in the heart of India. Growing up, Vizoto had never imagined that one day he would be guarding this place of devotion and reverence. And yet, the brave blood of his ancestors prompted him to rise to the occasion and put up a determined resistance against those who wanted to wreak havoc in the country.

Bravery, in the field, also means a presence of the mind. There is a very thin line between life and death. Courage also means being able to act on intuition and reflexively acting on all that had been learnt. It also means being able to ensure the safety of the citizens of the country. Today, Vizoto is a role model for many. "I was only doing my duty," he shrugs very modestly.

□

यथा ह्येकेन चक्रेण न रथस्य गतिर्भवेत्।
एवं परुषकारेण विना दैवं न सिद्ध्यति।।

Like a chariot cannot move with one wheel,
similarly, efforts cannot yield results without destiny.

Valour in Adversity

DHARAMBIR SINGH

Dharambir glanced at his watch as he made his way towards the Sita Rasoi. His sharp eyes noticed the sentry wiping his brow and resolved to ensure that the position of the fan should be changed in the afternoon. Dharambir was the Coy Havildar Major of the Jawans who were on duty at the sensitive Ram Janmabhoomi-Babri Masjid in Ayodha. As CHM (Company Havildar Major), it was his duty not just to ensure that the sentries were alert and the men performed well, but also to see that they were comfortable in doing so. The sand-filled sentry posts had tin roofs on which the July sun beat down mercilessly. It was mid-morning and the usual crowd of devotees wound their way towards the *garbha griha* or the sanctum sanctorum.

Ayodhya, the city revered by many across the nation, had a special place in the security scenario of the country. When Dharambir first came to the dusty temple town, he had carried with him the childhood impressions of the time which was interspersed with mentions of the glory of Ayodhya. This was the city where Lord Rama has established the Ramrajya. Ayodhya derived its name from a *yudh* or a 'city of no wars'. And yet, here he was, on his way to a place on duty with the CRPF to ensure the security of the same legendary city of the epic Ramayana.

Growing up in Sehlangh village of Mahendergarh district, Dharambir was enrolled at the local Government Middle School. It was a small village where less than a thousand families resided. His father was a farmer. With five brothers and two sisters, the family struggled to make the two ends meet. When the elder sister married and moved to Pratapur in Rajasthan, Dharambir moved with her. It was here that he fell in love with sports, excelling in volleyball. It also opened up the world to him. Physical fitness and an enduring respect for nutrition followed.

His sister had been married to a handsome man. This new addition to the family was employed with the CRPF. Dharambir was impressed by the tales of bravery of CRPF men. Hence when he learnt of an open recruitment to the force taking place in Avadi, Chennai, he borrowed money from his sister and appeared for the exams. Clearing the exams effortlessly, he was directed to join at 83 Bn CRPF, which was being raised at Bhubaneswar within the next ten days. He was so elated that he didn't even realise that there wasn't enough time to meet his family at Mahendergarh, before reporting for duty. He had been married only four months ago and now would meet his new wife six months later, but this time in a uniform during the mid-term break.

His first experience of dealing with militancy arrived soon. He was deployed with the 55 Bn located at Chudachandpur in Manipur. The tough terrain, inclement weather conditions,

HEROES
WILL RISE

poor systems of communication and bad living conditions honed the soldier in him and prepared him for the life ahead. When militancy raised its head in Punjab, his unit was rushed to Bhatinda. In the annual changeover of troops, Dharambir was sent to Kalimpong near Darjeeling where the troops faced a different kind of hostility. The next few years and exigencies of service took him to Abohar on the border with Pakistan and then to Kashmir Valley. He also served at Noonmati, Guwahati and Lalwas, Jaipur. He earned his rank as head constable in 2003 and was posted to 33 Bn at Doda, Jammu & Kashmir. After completion of duties in a tough terrain, the unit was moved to a comparatively soft posting at Ayodhya.

Ayodhya was considered as 'soft posting' for many reasons. It is located in the heartland of the country and is easily accessible. Compared to other CRPF locations, it did not have the same threat perception and armed encounters were not commonplace. The local populace was not hostile and one did not really need armed escorts on routine movements. The markets were accessible and one's family could also pay a visit. It was precisely because of these perceptions that the officers did not allow the personnel to lower their guard. Briefings and regular exercises ensured that the personnel on duty were sharp and alert. As Coy Havildar Major, Dharambir had an additional responsibility and he was very aware about this. On him rested the responsibility of assigning tasks suitable to the personnel of the company. To meet this expectation, he had to personally know each man and his weaknesses and strengths. He also had to know them intimately so as to be aware of the issues faced by each of them in their professional and private lives. A CRPF company is very closely knit; the CHM keeps it together. It is a very prestigious assignment with its own privileges and responsibilities. It is also very sought after and the CHM is selected very carefully by the officers. Dharambir took his job very seriously. He looked towards the sentry at Sita Rasoi and noted with satisfaction that the latter stood alert. He scanned the crowd yet again to look for aberrations; there were none.

The Ramjanmabhoomi had caught the imagination of the country in the preceding years. It had been at the political crosshairs of the Indian landscape and had become a very sensitive issue which had the possibility to arise communal passions. Following the incident of December 6, 1992, a makeshift structure had been erected. This 2.77 acres of land was heavily guarded by the Central Reserve Police Force. Divided into various zones, a three-tier security cordon was thrown around it. Dharambir's company was in the innermost cordon and he reviewed it yet again. It was 9 a.m. and the crowds were liable to recede by 11 a.m. when the summer sun would scorch the dusty land.

Suddenly there was a huge blast that shattered the peaceful environs and reverberated across the place. The source of such a sound was nor clear. The walkie-talkie sets started a jumbled conversation. Dharambir quickly moved to ascertain the source of the sound. Before he could really move, the unmistakable sound of automatic gunfire erupted again from the same direction. Years of training kicked in and reflexively he removed the safety catch of his weapon. The body and machine were ready to take on the terrorists.

The wireless sets were now clearer and providing information. The outer barricade had been breached by some armed terrorists, who had used an explosive-laden jeep to ram into it. They were trying to reach the isolation zone of the *parisar* (campus). This was where Dharambir's company was deployed. Very calmly he noticed that the coy had come to stand-to position; the contingency drill was set into motion. He also noticed that the CRPF Jawans were now scanning the landscape to look for the terrorists. The safety and security of the pilgrims was foremost on their mind.

Dharambir crawled towards, the *morcha*, which was a sentry post made of sand bags at Sita Rasoi, where Constable Om Prakash was already in a tactical position and ready to fire at the terrorists. He started a long crawl towards the *morcha*, which seemed to be under direct onslaught of the terrorists. He could clearly see them firing but held his own fire as there were pilgrims, who could have been hit. Once he reached the makeshift *morcha* of sandbags, he noticed that it was confronting the incoming fire bravely. Suddenly, a grenade exploded next to the *morcha*, damaging one side completely. He also noticed that the ground next to him had begun to turn red. Perplexed, he looked around and was surprised to see it was his own blood that was seeping to the ground. Omprakash looked at the wound sustained by his CHM (Company Havildar Major). In a silent communication, he tied a handkerchief around his superior's wound and then they set to work. The task before them was much bigger than any such wound. The communal harmony of the country was at stake and they stood between the nefarious designs of the terrorists. The attack had to be foiled. The steely resolve of the CRPF was facing a test; they could not fail. Their weapons opened fire in retaliation in order to halt the terrorists in their track.

Their Coy Commander, Tinyi had reached them by now. The reinforcements had also started to move towards the *parisar*. A fierce gun battle ensued. When the fire stopped, Dharambir got up wearily and came to know that two CRPF personnel were injured. All the five terrorists had been eliminated. They failed to breach the sanctity of the

Ramjanmabhoomi. As CHM, he wanted to meet his Jawans and speak to them in greater detail. However, the wound was throbbing with pain and the handkerchief was soaked in blood. The officers insisted on his seeking medical aid; hence he reluctantly left the site. As the ambulance wound its way, carrying the injured H.C. Dharambir, the sirens seemed to proclaim the victory of good over evil–the concept that his mother had taught him years ago and the values that the CRPF stood for.

The Shaurya Chakra is awarded for bravery and valour in the face of adversity when facing perils to one's life. Dharambir was awarded this medal for his unflinching devotion to duty and for standing up to adversity. He received the award from the President of India, Dr. A.P.J. Abdul Kalam in a glittering ceremony at the Rashtrapati Bhawan. As he marched up to the dais to receive the award, the hall erupted into applause and his wife of many years watched him with pride and tears in her eyes. She had raised the children single handedly as Dharambir had to move across the country, from one conflict area to another. She wasn't really sure if she understood the complexities of the areas where he was deployed but this one moment made it seem all worth it. For the Defence Investiture Ceremony she had received a personal invitation and was accommodated at the Ashoka Hotel. She was being treated like royalty as she memorised every small detail to narrate to her friends back home.

Today the children have grown up and Dharambir is serving at Delhi. He plans to hang up his boots soon and go back to the village where his family awaits his return. July 5, 2005 remains etched in his memory and the medal on his chest glitters as he proudly adorns his uniform every day.

□

उत्साहो बलवानार्य नास्त्युत्साहात्परं बलम्।
सोत्साहस्य च लोकेषु न किंचिदपि दुर्लभम्॥

Enthusiasm is the power of noble men.
Nothing is as powerful as enthusiasm.
Nothing is difficult in this world for
an enthusiastic person.

The Jungle Warrior

ASHISH KUMAR TIWARY

It was a sultry July evening. The last rays of the sun had tinged the sky and the troops of 202 CoBRA unit were winding up the day's work. A volleyball game was in progress. Generally, the officers and men join together to play with enthusiasm. Deputy Commandant Uday Divyanshu, the commander of the camp, had been called away. An urgent message awaited him. As Uday walked back, he went over the details of what he had learnt.

Commando Battalion for Resolute Action or CoBRABns is a specialised battalion of the Central Reserve Police Force. Raised in 2008, the personnel are selected and put through rigorous training in guerrilla warfare before being inducted into the CoBRA units. These are tough boys who are ready to fight in the rough terrain of dense jungles. Miles away from their homes, these boys take on the Naxals, who are perpetually engaged in a deadly war. Uday and his troops belonged to the 202 CoBRA which was deployed in west

Midnapore. The CoBRA camp was close to two habitations– the Adivasipara and Kamyapara.

Intelligence inputs indicated that a Naxal party had visited the village to enjoy dinner and then left for the jungles towards the east. The jungles in the vicinity were very dense, hence, the Naxals could not have gone too far. The CoBRA forces decided to launch an operation to take them on. It was late evening of July 25, 2010 when the party left for the jungles. They had to move stealthily in the dense foliage; swiftly and carefully manoeuvring their way through the vegetation. A narrow path marked the trail which the villagers took, but the CoBRA boys knew this path wasn't safe enough; hence they had to negotiate their way through the rough terrain. Moonlight showed the way which meandered through the undergrowth. The fertile rich soil on the banks of Kangsabati river led to green cover, with tall sal trees forming the forest on the Dalma hills. These hills constitute a part of the Bengal-Jharkhand Range. Elephants are a common sight in the area. The troops had covered only a short distance when a slight drizzle began. In the dim light, the troops pushed ahead.

Located on the banks of Kangsabati river, Midnapore has been witness to Left-wing extremism. Popularly known as the city of tribal tradition, Midnapore derives its name from the local deity, Midini Mata, who is believed to be an incarnation of Shakti. Historically, this place was held by Siraj-ud-Daulah who was betrayed by Mir Jafar on 20 June 1757. This betrayal to the East India Company led by Robert Clive at Plassey consolidated the hold of the Company on India and changed the course of Indian history forever. Years later, the city redeemed itself by rising against the British in the Santhal Revolt and the Chuar rebellion. In a violent turn of events, three British District Magistrates were murdered

COBRA
JUNGLE WARRIORS
COBRA

in succession by the revolutionaries. Khudiram Bose was sentenced to death for a failed attempt to kill Magistrate Kingsford. Independence brought development and peace. However, the area had been restive for some years now.

They walked the entire night and approached the area where the Naxals were expected to be camping. The detailed plan was now put into action. The area under search was approximately 1 km in width and 2 km long. The inputs were quickly collated once again and the troops were adequately briefed. A three-pronged approach was adopted. The central axis was to be led by Assistant Commandant, Pancham Lal aided by Constables Ashish Tiwari, S.Y. Reddy, Lal Bahadur while Sub-Inspector Mangla Prasad and Head Constable Sri Kishen were to move from the left. Personnel from Goaltore police station were to cover the right flank.

It was the darkest hour of the night when the troops spotted a rust-coloured tent pitched close to the ground. They were almost certain that it belonged to the Naxals who might have been resting after the trek. Very cautiously the troops cordoned the area. Ashish Tiwari was part of the central axis team. Essentially, his task was to ensure that the insurgents are unable to break the cordon and flee. A shy, introvert, young boy, Ashish had joined the unit very recently. CRPF units are close-knit teams. The boys spend long durations of time in the units and develop affinity for each other over a period of time. This close bonding is also an operational necessity. In operations, laced with complexities, even small errors can lead to far-reaching consequences; hence one must know the team members intimately. Tasks are assigned on the basis of individual strengths and weaknesses. An in-depth analysis is a must. People work in a 'buddy system' with the second man complementing the first. This age-old system has stood the test of time and is followed religiously. Forces work on mutual trust. Hailing from Jharkhand, Ashish gelled into the team quickly. Nimble on his feet, he was physically fit and passionate about his work. The officers had selected him to be part of the tightly-knit group.

Once the teams were in place, the striking team crawled up to the rust-coloured tent where the Naxals were relaxing. Close by, a Naxal sentry dozed under the shelter of broad leaves. The drizzle had now taken the form of proper rain. The CoBRA commandos crept closer. Suddenly, the Naxals realised that they had been surrounded. They opened gunfire. The stillness of the night was broken by the sound of the bullets whizzing past. There was utter chaos. A pitched gun-fight ensued. In the midst of this, a woman's shrill voice rang out. She was asking for mercy. Ashish raised his hand to ask his colleagues to stop firing. The troops stopped the fire immediately. A Naxal hand appeared from behind the tent flaps and shot at the troops from point blank range. Ashish was ready and retaliated almost immediately. Then the brave trooper fell. The guns soon fell silent. An eerie silence descended.

As dawn broke over the horizon, Uday and Pancham realised the enormity of what lay before them. A stretcher was quickly made and a grievously hurt Ashish was sent to the nearest camp for medical aid. The road ahead was a 6-km trek which the bearers covered as quickly as possible. A single bullet had pierced below Ashish's ear. He suffered from heavy blood loss but his companions rested on hope and miracle. The dreaded Naxal, Sidhu Soren had been eliminated along with five other Naxals. A huge cache of arms and ammunition along with incriminating Naxal literature were also recovered.

When the exhausted party reached the camp that night, a pall of gloom descended. Ashish had fallen prey to the gunshots, making the supreme sacrifice of his life at the altar of duty. His friends spoke of him in glowing terms and gave him a hero's farewell. As his mortal remains lay in state at the Quarter Guard, his colleagues and close comrades filed past.

Miles away, in Garwah, Jharkhand, the news of his heroism and sacrifice reached his parents. Ashish had been home only a month earlier. His father, a farmer, lived with his two sons and a daughter in Attawala, a small hamlet on the outskirts of Garwah. The children had been enrolled at the Government High School. Ashish was a good student and had graduated from the Ramdhari College. When CRPF launched the recruitment drive at Daltonganj, Palamu, in 2006, Ashish applied and was selected. He joined for duty at Koraput, Odisha and spoke in high terms of the Force he had joined. In the locality, he was a role model. The boys were fond of him and many others too wanted to join the Force. In June 2010, he had returned home on one month's leave. The elder brother was getting married and it was time for a celebration. After the celebrations, when he was leaving, Ashish informed the family that he had been selected to be part of the elite CoBRA Bn of the CRPF. The family did not know much about CoBRA but were aware that it was a privilege to be part of it. He was to join the unit on 25 June.

The trains on the Latehar route had been cancelled due to a strike and the family advised Ashish to extend his leave, but Ashish did not agree and instead chose to proceed to his destination by road. They could not have realised that it was to be his last visit home.

The Shaurya Chakra is awarded for outstanding bravery in the face of imminent danger. Ashish had exhibited raw courage in a situation which led to elimination of Sidhu Soren, who was part of the group of the Silda offensive in which 25 Jawans of the Eastern Frontier Rifles were killed. Soren, or Bhuta Baskey, was one of the founder members of the People's Committee against Police Atrocities and the chief of the Sidhu-Kanhu Gana Militia–the armed wing of the Maoists. He also headed the Goltore squad which came to be dreaded in the years to come. The encounter was a watershed in the history of anti-Naxal operations in Midnapore as the Naxal menace started dwindling thereafter with the Naxals being on the run and with the security forces turning on the heat upon them. Ashish's parents received the Shaurya Chakra on his behalf and as expected, it occupies a place of pride and honour in his home. He had lived up to the motto of CoBRA–'*Sangrame parakrami jyee*' (Victory for the gallant in war).

□

अकर्तव्यं न कर्तव्यं प्राणैः कण्ठगतैरपि।
कर्तव्यमेव कर्तव्यं प्राणैः कण्ठगतैरपि॥

Works which has been entrusted
with responsibility have to be achieved by all means.

Invincible Spirit

R.K. SINGH

Ravindra Kumar Singh looked at the dark sky and concluded that it would take another half hour for daybreak. Mentally he re-assessed his plan for the day. Singh was commanding the Foxtrot coy of the 133 Bn of the Central Reserve Police Force. The base camp was at Lohardaga. The previous evening, Singh had received an intelligence input on the presence of Maoists. At the break of first light of dawn, he would lead his team of more than 120 men of the F/133, 94Bn and a platoon of Jharkhand Armed Police to the hills of Hurmur and Ganeshpur. Singh had been in charge of this area for a couple of months. He knew the operation was wrought with risks and therefore, mentally reassessed his plan.

Lohardaga is a small town in Jharkhand state. Located west of the state capital of Ranchi, the district is famous for its bauxite mines. Etymologically, its name is derived from two Hindi words–*lohar* (ironsmith) and *daga* (centre). Thus, the literal meaning is 'centre of iron mining'. The mining town has also been a flourishing base for Maoists with the Red Corridor passing through it. Spanning across 11 states and affecting more than 90 districts, the area witnesses sporadic bursts of violence. These densely populated areas also suffer from poverty, illiteracy and under-development. Agriculture, sometimes supplemented by mining or forestry, is the mainstay of economy. Non-diversification into other enterprises has led to a situation where the economy is unable to support the rapid increase in population. Caste and feudal divisions abound in the area. The area has a high concentration of indigenous tribal population or 'Adivasis', including the Santhals and the Gonds. In fact, the Red Corridor stretches from the Nepal border to the fringes of the southern state of Tamil Nadu. Singh had read about the concept of the Revolutionary Base Area. He knew that Maoists had carved out a base area as a local stronghold in a remote mountainous area or a forest with a difficult terrain so that the enemy would find it difficult to navigate and attack. The revolutionary movement was able to muster broad local support against the better equipped government forces.

Against this backdrop, Singh went over the plan drawn for the day. The Dhardharia forest lay in between the route. The troops were well armed and prepared for action. They had to cover the distance during the day, search the area and return to the base by the evening. He had marked the route on the maps and briefed his men the day before. At daybreak, they were prepared to leave. Singh thought of calling his wife to wish her as it was her birthday. He picked up the phone to dial a call but then thought better of it. It was too early; he would call later. Picking up his assault rifle instead, he left.

Singh wanted to cover the distance as swiftly as possible as the summer sun would soon be overhead. The dry day

would make walking difficult. It was a forested area with a hilly terrain and the men had to be cautious too. The place was dotted with small villages, like Sake and Hurmur, which had a population of less than a thousand each. It was a picturesque place where only the chirping of birds punctuated the silence. Singh knew they could not let down their guard but the environs were relaxing. Just as they were moving towards village Sake, on the northeastern part of Hurmur, a series of explosions ripped apart the silence. Singh was thrown in the air by the impact of the explosion and was momentarily disoriented. When he came to his senses, the air was still thick with dust and explosions could be heard all around. He quickly realised that the troops had been ambushed. He made an attempt to get up but was held to the ground by his buddy and team-mate, Constable Dhaula. Mentally assessing the situation and drawing up an evacuation and counter-drill to the attack, Singh realised that something was gravely wrong with him. He saw that his left leg was bleeding profusely. He looked again, found the left foot missing. Realising that the foot must have been blown off, he looked incredulously. Amazed that he couldn't feel the pain, it dawned on him that the body was in a state of shock. Reflexively he turned to his buddy and gave detailed instructions on how to tie a tourniquet. The blood loss had to be stemmed. One of his men tore away the pants while another tied it up. In the absence of anything suitable, they used a shoelace to stem the loss of blood. There was a look of horror and compassion on the face of Constable Dhaula. By now, the Naxals were firing on the pinned-down troops.

Suddenly the firing stopped and a voice conveyed in an intimidating voice over the mike that the troops should lay down their weapons and surrender.

Singh felt an overpowering emotion course through his body–a feeling of outrage! The soldier in him reacted with every fibre of his being. Every nerve pulsed and every vein stood alert. In a powerful voice, he responded by challenging the insurgents and let fly a slew of bullets. The sound echoed over the hills. His own hitherto demoralised troops responded to his clarion call. A pitched gunfight ensued.

Soon the insurgents beat a hasty retreat. As the last sound of gunfire died down, Singh crawled to his fellow troopers. He knew many had laid down their lives at the altar of duty but there were some others, who lay grievously injured. He wanted to arrange for their evacuation to the hospital. There were many who had sustained injuries on their eyes. To him, it seemed that their injuries were more important.

He messaged an SOS and reinforcements reached to evacuate the injured. Rabindra was wrapped in a blanket and lifted to safety. Ultimately, the exhausted body could take no longer. Weary but satisfied that he had done his best, Singh collapsed in the arms of his fellow trooper.

Miles away, Singh's wife, Ratna, awaited his call on her special day. She wasn't unduly annoyed. Aware that his job often took him to the interiors of the jungles of Jharkhand, where the connections were erratic at best, she waited for the birthday wishes. She was a teacher of chemistry in the local college and had missed the news of the attack. When the usual call did not materialise till 11 p.m., she had a deep sense of foreboding. She called her husband's fellow trooper and learnt the news. Singh had been grievously injured and had been airlifted to Apollo Hospital at Ranchi. She bore the news stoically. A true leader's wife, she enquired about the troops and then requested to speak with her husband.

Ravindra was nonchalant about his injuries. He told her

it was just a bruise and he was only visiting because of the troops. He tried not to divulge any information about the extent of his injuries. Ratna patiently heard her husband trying to lie to her. Very composed, she informed him that she was on her way to Ranchi as she knew he was in the ICU at Apollo Hospital. Rabindra smiled and hung up. He no longer had to lie to the person who knew him so well.

Sometime later, she gently broke the news of his injury to their young son and also to his old parents. Then it was time to take the flight to Ranchi. As the flight landed, she braced herself for a long struggle ahead.

In another part of the country, Ravindra's father, Brijender Singh, was deeply disturbed at the news of his son's injuries. A deep sense of unrest kept telling him that something was amiss; maybe they weren't telling him the complete story. He kept pestering people for nuggets of news but there wasn't much forthcoming. He had retired as a District Judge some years earlier. Professional calling had taken him to various parts of the state. His four sons had accompanied him on these transfers. Rabindra was born in Firozabad and had a streak of independent thought and action. While his other sons had taken up the legal profession, this son had been different. Ever since he had enrolled for NCC Scouts at school, following his passion while studying at the Government Inter College, Unnao, he had expressed a desire to join the CRPF. A graduate from PPN College, Kanpur, he enrolled at the Dept. of Laws at Allahabad University. The elder Singh had hoped that the exposure would steer Ravindra towards the legal profession but the city had a different impact on him.

The rich history of the place and its intersectionality with India as a nation had left a deep mark on Ravindra. The city's original name, Prayag, meant 'a place of offerings.' It is mentioned in the Vedas as the location where the Lord of Creation, Brahma, had attended a ritual sacrifice. The city finds mention in the *Puranas* as the place where Yayati was based and left to conquer the Sapta Sindhu. His five sons–Yadu, Druhyu, Puru, Anu and Turuvashu–had founded the five main tribes as mentioned in the Rigveda. The city was called Kaushambi and was the capital of the Kuru rulers who shifted from Hastinapur when it was destroyed by floods. Located at the confluence of the Ganga, Yamuna and Saraswati rivers, the city had been the political, cultural and administrative centre of the Doab. A succession of dynasties and empires followed. The Maratha incursions and attack by Mohammed Ghori prompted the Mughal emperor, Akbar to call it Ilahabad or 'place of Gods'. The year 1765 marked a turning point for the city when the combined forces of Indian princes lost the Battle of Buxar to the British. This was followed by the Treaty of Allahabad and the establishment of a British garrison at the Allahabad Fort. In 1801, the city was ceded to the British.

In the streets of Allahabad resound the stirring stories of the freedom struggle even today and underline the importance of the city. On a visit to the Madan Mohan Malviya Park, Ravindra had learnt of its importance. Allahabad was a major participant in the Revolt of 1857 which shook the very foundations of the British in India. Maulvi Liaquat Ali had raised the banner of freedom in the city. He was amazed to learn of the story that unfolded in January 1858 and led to the establishment of the British Empire in India. Earl Canning departed from Calcutta to reach Allahabad. At Minto Park, he read Queen Victoria's proclamation transferring control of India from the East India Company to the British Crown. This marked the beginning of the British Raj in India.

The city was to later witness the 1888 session of the

Indian National Congress. It also became a centre for the revolutionaries. Nityanand Chatterji hurled a bomb at the European Club here. In 1931, Chandershekhar Azad died at Alfred Park when he was surrounded by the British. His visits to the Anand Bhavan and the Swaraj Bhavan, which were epicentres of political activity for a long time, left a deep imprint on the young man. While the city was home to many *satyagrahis* as well, it saddened him that the seeds of the two-nation theory were also sown here. It was here on December 29, 1930 that Allama Muhammad Iqbal, in his presidential address to the All India Muslim League, proposed a separate Muslim State for the Muslim-majority regions of the country. This was a living heritage and he vowed to protect it.

Ravindara's father understood that powerful emotions drive people to great heights. So, when Rabindra told him of his passion and sought permission to join the CRPF, The father agreed, albeit reluctantly. He did not want to hurt the sentiments of his son. Keeping his fears at bay, he had acquiesced to the son's wishes. Ravindra did not disappoint. He was selected for deputation to the elite National Security Guards where he excelled as a Black Commando. He was picked up for the Special Protection Group that provides security to the Prime Minister. Here he performed equally well. When he went to the jungles of Jharkhand to challenge the Maoist menace, his father was not unduly worried. But now, this devastating piece of news! He was very deeply affected in his old age. As he prayed for the safety of his son, he remembered his promise to his late wife that Ravindra would never make a wrong move. He went over his rosary yet again.

In the hospital, the medical officers fought to save Ravindra. The tourniquet that his companion had strung on the left leg had done its job. The loss of blood was a concern but a bigger factor loomed. By the time Ravindra was moved from the jungles to the hospital, gangrene had set in. To save his life, the leg had to be amputated. There was no other option. Ratna, his wife, did not flinch. Calmly she nodded her consent. With a heavy heart, the doctors set to save the life of the brave soldier.

On May 5, the brave warrior underwent amputation of the left leg just below the knee. After a hospitalisation period of twenty days, he was ready to fly home to Delhi. As they wheeled him out at Delhi Airport, a cheer went up within the CRPF. Our brave soldier was home. The Director General, CRPF, K. Vijay Kumar, had made sure that best medical treatment was extended to him. The Army medical officers, with immense experience in dealing with trauma injuries, had stepped in. Under the close supervision of Army Base Hospital, New Delhi, Ravindra's wounds healed remarkably. They also mentioned that Endolite India, a prosthetic company based in Naraina, New Delhi could help in fitting an artificial limb. Some people had feared that Rabindra would baulk at the prospect of a prosthetic limb. They were in for an amazing response. He actually looked forward to the fitting and testing his willpower.

The injured stump generally takes weeks to adjust to the prosthetic. Similarly, the mind is known to play games as it seeks to adjust to the absence of a limb. Rabindra had his apprehensions but kept them to himself. He didn't know what to expect, yet looked forward to regaining mobility. On the second day of the fitting, the doctors told him that they would try the fitting and he could put weight on the leg. He was cautioned not to overdo or to be overambitious. They kept telling him to keep safety first as many people tend to treat the prosthetic as a normal leg. This is wrong on many counts, but the basic issue is that the brain passes instructions to the foot. However, this is impossible with a prosthetic. The person is therefore liable to fall and sustain injuries. Any injury in this state can make things very difficult, they said. He was fitted with a prosthetic leg and taken to a room with parallel bars. He was to try to walk very carefully between the bars. As he looked around the room, he saw a young child of five walking on a prosthetic limb. Rabindra was mesmerised. 'If this child can do it, so can I', he thought. 'I am a trained soldier with a brave life behind me. I can surely do this.' With renewed determination, and a smile, he tapped his new leg and rose to begin a new chapter in his life.

In the intervening months, the CRPF transferred him to Group Centre, Noida. In July, the officers called up and asked him to join if he wanted to. Rabindra refused; Ratna could not comprehend this. She knew he missed office life. She was also aware that the Force had his best interests in mind. She tried to convince him to rejoin, knowing that the idea was to return to the normal office routine. Ravindra refused to reconsider his decision; instead he increased his time at the local gym. One evening, sweating profusely, he explained the rationale to her. He wanted to go to office, walking unescorted without any assistance. He would have to join, attired in civil clothes, on a wheelchair–this was unacceptable to him. Quietly, he requested the department to extend his leave.

Soon the appointed day arrived. Ravindra woke up early. He dressed quietly and then walked to the waiting official car. Ratna, the strong woman, who had stood by her husband's side steadfastly, without a trace of sadness but with a steely resolve, waved at the departing car. Then she broke down and cried her heart out. Her soldier was back at work.

The Shaurya Chakra is awarded for valour, courage and

self-sacrifice in the line of duty. Rabindra's life has been all this and more. At the Defence Investiture Ceremony, held at the Ashoka Hall of Rashtrapati Bhavan in New Delhi, Rabindra walked up to the then President, Smt. Pratibha Patil. He smartly saluted the Supreme Commander of the Armed Forces, who pinned the medal which epitomises bravery and courage.

Rabindra has gone on to participate in competitive table tennis and badminton at the Force-level tournaments. He has trekked in the hills and driven his family in a Wagon-R from Delhi to Khardungla Pass in Leh. The adventure enthusiast participated in a cycling expedition from Manali to Khardungla, in 2016. He also cycled from Itanagar to Mechuka in Arunachal Pradesh, in 2018. The spirit does not allow him to give up. Ravindra quotes Anais Nin, an unconventional writer and poet, who said, "Life shrinks or expands according to one's courage."

□

उद्यमः साहसं धैर्यं बुद्धिः शक्तिः पराक्रमः।
षडेते यत्र वर्तन्ते तत्र देव सहायकृत्।।

If the six qualities of industriousness, Capacity to make strenuous efforts, courage, patience, intelligence, power and courage, exist in a person, even the God Almighty renders assistance to him.

Courage under Fire

NAGENDRA SINGH

Assistant Commandant Nagendra Singh looked up from his laptop. The glance was sufficient to convey the query in his eyes. DIG Vineet Goel looked at the Google Earth window in front of him, carefully scanned the paper map, thought for a moment and nodded his assent. The third officer, Assistant Commandant Vinoj Joseph gave his consent too. The plan seemed good enough. In the circumstances, this was the best. They did not have the luxury of time to make a detailed plan. This would have to do.

Nagendra worked as a Company Commander with the Central Reserve Police Force. When the CRPF raised the elite CoBRA or the Commando Battalion for Resolute Action to counter the Naxalite terror, Nagendra was selected. A three-month rigorous training followed. In 2010, he was posted to 207 CoBRA which was deployed in the Jungle Mahal area of west Midnapore.

Barely half an hour ago, Nagendra had received a call

from the Superintendent of Police, West Bengal. He had shared a sensitive information and wanted to know if they could launch an operation. Nagendra knew that this would be difficult. The troops were away on an area-domination exercise with Assistant Commandant Vinoj Joseph. It had been a three-day exercise and the troops would return tired and exhausted. However, the source of the intelligence input was a reliable one. Nagendra had a quick word with his Commandant, Shri D.T. Banerjee and decided to follow through with the information. When Vinoj returned, he insisted on going along. Nagendra was pleased with this turn of events. Given the sensitivity of the information and the area, a greater strength would be beneficial.

It was late afternoon of 24 November, 2011 when the troops set off from their camp at PS west Midnapore. The ASP Jhargram, Alok Rajouriya was with them along with the troops of the State Armed Police. They had carefully gone over the information available and also the plan. The elusive Kishenji was known to be in the area along with Suchitra Mahato. They carefully studied a recent photo of Kishenji. There were very few snaps available of the Maoist leader; this, however, was a recent one. A well-known fact was that Kishenji was hard of hearing and used a hearing aid.

Mallojula Koteswara Rao, also known as Kishenji, was also known as the 'face' of the Maoist movement in India. Nagendra's mind went back to all he had read on Kishenji. Born into a poor family in Peddapalli, Karimnagar district of Tamil Nadu, Kotanna, as he was fondly known, Kishenji was a bright student. Despite his limitations, he graduated from SSR College at Warangal in 1973. A year later, he went underground. He believed that independence from the British had strengthened the ruling rich and had failed to bring about

change in the lives of the tribal people. Kishenji had joined the Telangana Sangharsh Samiti and later founded the Radical Students Union (RSU). The peasant movement of Karimnagar's Jagitial and Siricilla (1977) saw his active participation. The movement was the precursor to the establishment of the People's War Group (PWG) a few years later, by Kondapalli Seetharamaiah. Kishenji was a founder member of the PWG and a Politburo member. A multi-faceted personality, Kishenji was known to be tech savvy and could communicate in at least six languages–Hindi, English, Santhali, Bangla, Odia and Telugu. From 1982-86, he had worked on strengthening the movement in Andhra Pradesh as secretary of the Communist Party of India's (Marxist-Leninist) People's War Group. He later led its Dandkaranya unit. Reportedly, he moved to the northeast in 1992 and worked in active collaboration with the radical groups there.

Kishenji had been known to have moved to West Bengal in 2000, after spending years in the Naxal belt of Maharashtra and Chhattisgarh–on the border with Jharkhand at the Jungle Mahal area. Literally meaning the 'jungle estates', this was an area formed by British possessions and some independent chiefdoms. The area lay between Birbhum, Bankura, Midnapore and the hilly terrain of Chhota Nagpur. The area was known as Jungle Terry, which means a thickly forested region inhabited by tribes, like the Santhals. The year 2004 witnessed a major regrouping with Kishenji playing a major role in the merger of the PWG with the Maoist Communist Centre of India (MCCI). The government launched an offensive against the Naxalites in the Red Corridor. The Naxalite response was violent. Kishenji is said to have planned and executed the 2010 attack on the Silda camp in which 24 personnel of the Eastern Frontier Rifles were killed. Between

2009 and 2011, their writ ran large. More than 350 civilians and 50 security personnel, besides more than 80 Maoists, were killed in this period.

It was 04.00 p.m. by the time the troops reached the designated area. Immediately, the officers regrouped and set about the task of establishing cordons and cut off parties. They wanted to be very careful now. They were on the fringes of the Kushbani jungle. A small village named Burisole lay ahead with some agricultural land and a pond. Previous experience had told them that this was an ideal location for the Naxals. A village on the edge of the jungle gave them the opportunity to escape, if cornered.

Suddenly, the scout, Constable S. Srinu raised his hand. This meant he had spotted someone and was signaling caution. The parties immediately split in a pre-decided fashion. Nagendra was to lead from the centre while Vinoj and his party would cover the right axis. The left flank was to be covered by Rajouriya of the West Bengal Police. The parties made their move, encircling the suspects. Nagendra's party had reached very close to the suspects. He could see them clearly and they appeared to be local villagers. Suddenly, gunshots broke the late evening silence. The suspects had whipped out automatic weapons and were running and firing indiscriminately. Nagendra did not hesitate and fired at the man causing the mayhem. The Naxal slumped. By this time, his accomplices were making a determined bid to escape, taking advantage of the dark hour. Rajouriya and Vinoj, along with their party, followed them and later found four villagers in a bullock cart. The Naxals had managed to mingle with the villagers, who would not divulge any information. Under duress from the naxals, the locals feared for their lives.

When the gunfire stopped, the CRPF regrouped. The slain

Naxal was carefully checked. His automatic rifle and hearing aid along with a missing tooth pointed to his identity as Kishenji. The local authorities were informed and the mortal remains were accorded due honour and sent to the Jhargram hospital. He was later identified by former associate Soma Mandi and by Atindranath Dutta, who was a police officer held captive in 2009. Overlooking the winding up of the operation took up the major part of the day. Nagendra and his team decided to halt at the village for the night.

As he lay down on a makeshift bed, Nagendra realised he had forgotten to speak with his family and feared that they might be worried. Then he smiled at the incongruity of the thought–there would anyway be no mobile connectivity in this part of the country. Nagendra's mind went back to the meandering route his life had taken to bring him here to the jungles of rural India. He was born in a large joint family residing at Kharra, Chandauli in Uttar Pradesh. The family was very attached to the roots wherein values were more important than any materialistic object. Kharra is located in Sakaldiha tehsil. The small town has less than 100 houses and remains a tightly-knit community. His father was an engineer with the UP Department of Irrigation. He was transferred very often, so Nagendra's childhood memories were a collection of varied places and friends. He was an inquisitive child but extremely reluctant to go to school. The family wanted him to join the Saraswati Shishu Mandir at Deoria. It seemed unfamiliar and outside his comfort zone. The wailing child could not be cajoled to stay in school. His sister, 10 years his senior, stepped in. She explained that schools would provide him answers to a plethora of questions. Saraswati, she explained, was the Goddess of Learning, who would bless him with wisdom. She shared her recent knowledge on the meaning of their town, Deoria. Apparently, the word means 'a place where there are temples'. Nagendra smiled at the thought of the memory of how he was sent to school. A string of schools in varied towns followed, but the first school remains special. His sister remains a repository of knowledge for him.

He enrolled at the Kali Prasad Inter-College at Allahabad. Established in 1871, the boys' college was set up as a college to provide quality education to Kayasthas. In 1920, the British government under Sir Harcourt Butler acquired the institution. As Nagendra walked down its corridors, he could feel the history seep into its tradition. This was to make a lasting impression on the young boy. He also acquired an immense love for cricket in the years here. A gifted batsman, he would regularly organise tournaments. The demi-god of Indian cricket, Sachin Tendulkar, and his exploits were followed vividly. On his uncomfortable bed in the interiors of India, Nagendra could take comfort in the joy Tendulkar had brought to millions of Indians. He wished he could tell Tendulkar this one day.

He chose to pursue a degree from Poorvanchal University, opting for the correspondence course. This was to focus his energies on the competitive exams for the Central Armed Police Force. Conducted by the Union Public Service Commission every year, it is a tough examination, comprising a written test followed by a physical efficiency test which is to check the physical fitness–a pre-requisite for the arduous duties ahead. A series of medical tests later, the candidate faces the interview board. Nagendra managed to clear the exam in his second attempt and reported at the CRPF Academy in 2009. An year later, armed with knowledge and much fitter than before, he was deployed at Nowhatta, Srinagar. Nothing in the academy had prepared him to deal with the situation there. Sure, they had taught him field craft and mob control and had also familiarised him with the historical perspective of the situation. But, dealing firmly on the ground needed quick thinking, agility and a community connect. One also needs to gauge the mood of the mob and use force accordingly. There was a lot to learn as every day brought new challenges. He now understood the importance of 52 weeks of hard work at the Academy. A sharp officer, Nagendra soon developed traits that would help him in the years to come.

In 2010, the CRPF was inducting selected officers and men into the CoBRA units. This specialised force was being raised to take on the Naxal menace in central India. Nagendra was picked up and put through three months' rigorous training at the Training College, Coimbatore at the end of which he became very familiar with jungle life. He reported to 207 CoBRA in February 2011.

After a deep sleep on a rickety makeshift bed, Nagendra woke up to a day of hectic activity. Senior officers of the CRPF and the state police flew in. The elimination of Kishenji was hailed as a major achievement and the clean operation was highly appreciated. Nagendra's bravery, courage, leadership and presence of mind in the face of imminent danger was applauded. He was able to speak to his family much later. They had already learnt of the operation through the media which had reported the operation widely.

The Shaurya Chakra, the peace-time gallantry award was conferred on the brave officer on the occasion of the Independence Day in 2012. On a personal front, Nagendra married his batchmate and fellow CRPF officer, Manisha Pathak in June 2012. She accompanied Nagendra for the Defence Investiture Ceremony held at Rashtrapati Bhavan on 23rd March, 2013 where the Supreme Commander of the Armed Forces pinned the Shaurya Chakra on Nagendra.

Nagendra's moment of satisfaction came a year later. In 2014, the CRPF organised a half marathon in honour of its Martyrs. Nagendra was deployed in Delhi and an active participant. Sachin Tendulkar consented to be the chief guest at the event. Nagendra's wish was fulfilled that day when he was able to meet his role model and icon of millions. Sachin was humility personified in meeting the Shaurya Chakra awardee.

Today, Nagendra has gone back to Chhattisgarh where he is deployed with 231 Bn CRPF. He uses his experience and knowledge of the terrain to guide the young officers who have taken on the mantle to bring peace to the area.

□

विद्या विवादाय धनं मदाय, शक्तिः परेषां परिपीडनाय।
खलस्य साधोः विपरीतम् एतत्, ज्ञानाय दानाय च रक्षणाय।।

Wicked men misuse their power while Noble and righteous persons use their knowledge, wealth and power for spreading, charity and protection of others.

Fearless

VINOJ P. JOSEPH

As soon as the gunfire ceased, Vinoj Joseph peeped out carefully from his semi-concealed position and scanned the landscape before him. The silence was eerie. Even the birds had fallen silent. He motioned towards his buddy, who had taken his position behind a termite hill. Together they began a slow crawl towards the heap in the middle of the farmland. The 'heap' had been firing with automatic weapons towards them just a few moments ago. In the agricultural field ahead, crops swayed silently, oblivious to the mayhem that they had witnessed just a few moments ago. Towards their left, Assistant Commandant Nagendra's team had begun a similar move towards the field.

Assistant Commandant Vinoj P. Joseph of the 207 CoBRA Bn of the Central Reserve Police Force was leading his team in an operation based on a specific intelligence input in the jungles of the west Midnapore area of West Bengal. The area, commonly known as Jungle Mahal, was on the border with Jharkhand

and was known to be an area dominated by the Naxals. Jungle Mahal had never been a delineated area and was part of the Red Corridor, so named as it witnesses considerable Naxalite-Maoist insurgency. While these are areas which also suffer from illiteracy and poverty, Naxalism had raised its ugly head in these areas which span parts of Andhra Pradesh, Bihar, Jharkhand, Madhya Pradesh, Maharashtra, Telangana, West Bengal and eastern Uttar Pradesh. Tackling this hydra-headed problem was one of the major issues confronting the nation. It was in this backdrop that the Central Reserve Police Force had been entrusted the task of raising a specialised wing–the Commando Battalion for Resolute Action. Vinoj was one of the first officers to be selected for intensive training which was imparted at the Central Training College, CRPF, Coimbatore. The three-month training had focused on jungle training and field craft. There was a sustained focus on being able to live off the land while negotiating the wild terrain. To Vinoj, who had been born and brought up at Kottayam in Kerala, this was a new experience. Though he had always been physically fit, this training took him to new heights. He also understood the importance of mental toughness. This extra edge was to come in handy in the field.

Vinoj had returned from a gruelling three-day area-domination exercise in the morning when he learnt of the operation which was being undertaken. Apparently, there was a specific intelligence report on the presence of four to five Naxals in the area. The Additional SP of Jhagram, Shri Rajouriya, who was to accompany was there with the team joint operation to be undertaken shortly. His colleague, Nagendra, Assistant Commandant, was wary because they didn't have the necessary numbers. Vinoj had immediately volunteered to be part of the operation. They had walked the

jungles in complete silence to reach the suspected area. The cordon was in the process of being laid when the scout raised a hand. The party had split into the pre-decided formations with Vinoj approaching from the right flank, Nagendra from the centre and Rajouriya from the right. Vinoj couldn't see the scout from his position but he could make out that there were three-four people in the field. In the late evening, as the sun dipped below the horizon, he could only see the silhouettes framed against the skyline. Suddenly, one of them whipped out a weapon and gunshots rang out. Bullets whizzed past the startled troops. But then years of training kicked in and they too opened fire. A few minutes of chaos followed. The fire stopped as suddenly as it had started.

When Vinoj peered out of his position behind a termite hill, he could see the Naxalites fleeing. Without a second thought, he ran behind them; Rajouria too joined in. It was the edge of a jungle and the village Burisole was not far away. The escaping people faded from view but the duo kept up the chase. However, All they could find were three villagers on a bullock cart. Frustrated, they turned back and trudged to the slumped person in the field. Nagendra and his team had already reached the spot. A man lay, riddled with bullets, along with his automatic weapon. When they saw the hearing-aid, they realized that this could be the elusive Maoist leader–Kishenji.

The troops then decided to halt at the village for the night. The intelligence tip-off had asserted that Kishenji was in the area along with Suchitra Mahato. The search for the remaining three Naxalites was to continue the next day.

Vinoj was able to speak with his wife, later that night. She was overwhelmed to hear from him. The news and media were widely covering the incident. Kishenji was a prominent leader and his neutralisation meant a lot to the security forces. It was big news Vinoj had got married only two years ago, so the CRPF and the dangers that they faced were also new to the young lady. She cried with relief and pride simultaneously. The next call was to his mother. Miles away from the jungles of Bengal, Mrs Joseph was overcome with emotion. She taught English at the Holy Angels School in Ullar, which is a small town in Trissur district of Kerala. The value of bravery and courage inculcated in her wards was now bearing fruit. While her husband worked in Ernakulum, she had brought up the three siblings single-handedly with affection and discipline. When Vinoj had expressed his desire to join the CRPF as a Sub-Inspector in 2003, she had given her blessings. After a year-long training, Vinoj had moved to strife-torn Jammu & Kashmir in 2004. A brief stint in Kokrajhar followed. He picked up his first promotion as an Inspector and moved to Sopore, Kashmir. His quest for knowledge did not let him rest and he qualified the departmental examination to become a gazetted officer. His selection to CoBRA followed soon thereafter. As the mother reminisced on this and more about her son, she blessed him on his achievements and silently prayed for his safety.

The Shaurya Chakra is awarded for bravery and courage exhibited in peacetimes. The medal is a testimony of courage in testing times when lesser mortals would have wilted. Vinoj had shown nerves of steel under pressure and also the willingness to go the extra mile in face of danger. At the Defence Investiture Ceremony held at the Ashoka Hall of the Rashtrapati Bhavan, Vinoj P. Joseph was conferred the Shaurya Chakra by the President of India, Dr. Pranab Mukherjee. The applause that greeted his citation conveyed the feelings of a grateful nation.

□

न त्वहं कामये राज्यं न मोक्षं न स्वर्गं नापुनर्भवम्
कामये दुःखतप्तानां प्राणिनामार्तिनाशनम्

I do not desire kingdoms or State.
I do not want heaven or Moksha.
May I be helpful in eliminating pain and sufferings!

Valiant Warrior

PRAKASH RANJAN MISHRA

It was late September afternoon and Prakash Ranjan Mishra gazed at the undulating ground spread around. Acres of soothing green greeted his gaze. The solitude and the quiet hid many an undercurrent but for now, he let his gaze linger for some more time. The shrill sound of the mobile phone interrupted his reverie. The voice on the other side was soft but urgent. Special intelligence from a trusted source carefully explained about the probable presence of a team of naxals in the forested area just beyond Juri-Rabda, a village on the outskirts of Pratappur.

Mishra was an officer with the 203 CoBRA Bn of the Central Reserve Police Force. While the Unit HQr was at Barhi, Hazaribagh, the Company was located at Chatra. A decorated officer, he knew the area well and had been handpicked by the CRPF to operate in this difficult terrain. Thoughtfully, Mishra walked towards the command centre of his Unit. The probable area was far from his location and time was the essence. Also important was the secrecy of the mission, as and therefore the need to move immediately, tactically and in a manner that did not arouse any suspicion of any kind. Mishra knew that a lot was at stake here. He called for his trusted officers and shared part of the input. The mantra was to impart information on 'Need to know' basis. Quickly, the officers put together a team of 26 CoBRA commandos. The SDPO of PS Chatra joined them along with his team of 4 personnel of the Jharkhand Police. In no time, the party was ready to move. They chose to move in a truck as that would not arouse suspicion. By this time, night had begun to set in.

There was a long distance to cover as they had to travel from Chatra to Pratappur via Hunterganj. Chatra district forms part of the Hazaribagh plateau and while the soil is moderately fertile, the area is primarily dependent on rain fed agriculture. With sixty percent of the area under forest cover, the region is blessed with natural resources but is industrially under-developed. More than seventy five percent of the population lives below the poverty line. This is also an area affected by naxalism. Naxal training camps and Jan-adalats were are also common. In this backdrop, the Commando Battalion for Resolute Action (CoBRA) was raised to take on the Maoist challenge. While the units they had met success in many areas since their inception, large swathes of land still lay under the naxal grip. As of 2012, Chatra was one of the 14 highly affected districts in Jharkhand.

As the truck wound its way through the serpentine road over the undulating road, Mishra looked out and wondered at the land of his ancestors and what it had become. Mishra was born in a small village on the outskirts of Jehanabad. His father was the Headmaster of the local school and the

emphasis on education was consistent. The patriarch saw education as the silver boon to every situation and insisted that this was the only thing that could change lives. Prakash was the fourth born among five siblings and started his schooling from the local Govt. Primary School. This was followed by the Govt. Middle School, Amain which was located at some distance. For his matriculation, he had to enrol at the Govt. Higher Secondary School, Pandui. With less than eight hundred houses, Pandui is a small place but the school caters to a large area. Bihar School Education Board announced a dismal eleven percent pass percentage that year; Mishra was the only one to secure a First division in the school along with Distinctions in Maths and English.

Patna beckoned. Mishra moved to the capital city where his elder brothers were residing and preparing for various competitive examinations. He opted for Distance education for his Graduation as he wanted to focus on the exams which could guarantee employability. Soon he was selected for the post of Sub Inspector with the Central Reserve Police Force which he joined at Coimbatore in 1997. A series of transfers and deployments followed which took him to the conflict areas of Tripura and Kashmir. While he was with the elite Special Duty Group at New Delhi, he appeared for the Departmental exams for the post of Assistant Commandant. While he did not qualify in the first batch, the 2002 exams saw him through. He was put through intensive training at Pinjore and then at the Internal Security Academy, Mt Abu. Service conditons again took him to 136 Bn which was then deployed at Nalbari and Dibrugarh in Assam. In March 2005, he moved to Hazaribagh, Jharkhand.

As the truck lurched on towards its destination, Mishra reminisced his first brush with naxals. While returning from cordon and search operation which had been launched near Satbhini river in the intervening night of 30-31 Jan 2007, Mishra's party was ambushed. The naxals were well entrenched and had the advantage of surprise. The CRPF troops held on under Mishra's leadership and gave a befitting response. The naxals were forced to flee and a vast quantity of ammunition was recovered besides incriminating literature. Mishra's presence of mind and exceptional leadership under adverse circumstances was recognised and he was conferred with the Police Medal for Gallantry. The Unit again moved to Nalbari, Assam but Mishra's operational skills were noticed. On the recommendation of the then Director General of Police, Jharkhand, and the endorsement of DG CRPF, Mishra was brought back to Jharkhand and posted to 22 Bn CRPF.

July 28, 2008 brought another achievement wherein the party led by Mishra was successful in eliminating PLGA commander Niranjan Majhi along with his comrades. While the naxals were entrenched near Tilaiya village, Bishnugarh. Mishra was conferred with the President's Police Medal for Gallantry. On August 18, 2008, on receipt of specific information about the presence of naxals, Mishra and his party set out to comb the area of Noniadih and the forests adjoining Keredari. They were moving cross country avoiding the beaten track. Having crossed a river in spate and negotiating a thick vegetation, they observed a suspicious movement in a house. A heavy exchange of fire ensued which continued into the wee hours. The gun battle ended in the neutralisation of Kalia alias Suman Manjhi alias Parvez Da who was the Platoon commander of the MCCI Military Wing. Many other naxals were injured and arms & ammunition recovered besides more than one lakh rupees in Indian currency. For his conspicuous gallantry, courage and devotion to duty of a high order, Mishra was conferred with the First Bar to Gallantry. While this operation was still fresh, another intelligence input came on September 16, 2008. This was about the movement of CPI (M) activist of Krishna Yadav Group in the bordering area of Katkamsandi Police Station in Chatra. The troops walked the whole night in the thickly forested area and then waited for the first light. Suddenly, heavily armed naxals opened fire from both flanks. A fierce encounter followed with the troops under Mishra's command holding their ground. An exemplary command along with presence of mind and personal bravery earned Mishra his Second Bar to Police medal for Gallantry. On July 20, 2012, Mishra led the operation eliminating PLGA Regional commander, Ajay Ganjhu in Lakkarmana forest.

Mishra was brought out of his chain of thoughts by a sudden lurching of the vehicle. Something was amiss and not quite right. The driver had jumped out and was closely examining the truck's engine. He tried a few times but the vehicle just wouldn't move. As they couldn't afford to lose any more time, Mishra decided to flag down the next vehicle that appeared on the isolated road. It was late in the night and the traffic had slowed down to negligible by now. A mini bus appeared around the corner and the troops quickly shifted into it. However, there was a major issue at hand–the mini bus could not accommodate everyone. Mishra decided that they just couldn't wait for another vehicle to come or for the truck to be repaired. Hence it was decided that only 21 CoBRAs and 4 personnel of the Jharkhand Police would accompany Mishra.

It was 0130 am when the party reached the area which had been indicated by the informer. A major issue came up. They just couldn't establish any further contact with the informer.

This was important as they were in a thickly forested area with very little inhabitation. An attack here could be lethal. They again tried to establish a communication but failed. Suddenly Mishra thought of the brother of the informer and viola; he was able to guide them. The brother took them to a clearing in the jungle where they could make out the silhouette of a solitary house. It was pitch dark and only the jungle sounds could be heard in the distance. The warrior in Mishra knew something big was to happen tonight. The party decided to observe the house. However, the darkness was a major hindrance. Night vision devices proved to be of little help. Suddenly, there was a movement and they saw a woman and child come out of the hut. Mishra signalled the troops to stop in their tracks. There would be no operation as they did not want any civilian deaths or collateral damage. Mishra was convinced that the common man is just stuck between the naxals and the Forces. He wanted to avoid collateral damage at any cost. However, the lady moved away and the informer called to intimate that there were more than fifteen people inside the hut. Mishra asked his people to observe more closely and specially look for a sentry, if any could be spotted. The reply came as naught.

Mishra now decided to act. Quickly the parties distributed in the pre-decided format. Two parties covered from the flanks while three people were to take the centre. Mishra with Constable Balihar to his right and Constable Bunkar to his left moved. Stealthily, they approached the house. There was no visible movement till they reached. It was only upon reaching the house that they spotted the alert naxal sentry cancealed behind the door. However, he heard the movement and opened fire. This was very close range and Mishra felt a hail of bullets whizz past. Without a second thought, Mishra too opened fire. The naxal sentry slumped to the ground gasping. However, there was another burst from his right and Mishra felt a warm trickle at his neck. There was a searing pain in his right scapula. Mishra realised he had been hit. But there was no time to analyse or think any further. An intense gunfight broke out. In the darkness, Mishra could make out that people were scrambling out from the hut and fleeing into the forest area beyond. He could hear expletives and instructions being thrown around as the naxals tried to be beyond the reach of the Forces. One such burst had caught Constable Bunkar who was hit in the face. Mishra crawled up to his fallen comrade and forced a painkiller into his throat. There was blood spilled everywhere; Mishra could not even differentiate which part was his. Slowly he counted–he had been hit at atleast five places including in the thigh which throbbed painfully.

By this time, the fire had stopped and the troops regrouped. Mishra's concern was for Bunkar who was still bleeding profusely. Losing no time, he called his senior officers and briefed them. He also impressed upon the urgency making a chopper available.

Miles away, the phones starting ringing and urgent messages were flashed down the line. The killing of a dreaded naxal was a matter of satisfaction but some personnel were injured and needed immediate attention. The Air Force was requisitioned and the chopper was air-borne in no time. On the ground, the personnel administered first aid to their leader and colleague and started the long painful journey down a meandering path in the thick jungle. It was a slippery route when they had come; going back was harder as they carried the injured on make-shift stretchers. Every step was agony but time was also the essence and need of the hour. In the Control room, the officers noticed with dismay the thick clouds that had descended over the forest cover. The rescue had to be called off. With Mishra and the others needing expert medical care, another attempt was made by the Dhruv chopper which could evacuate successfully. It was late morning by the time, the injured personnel were at Apollo Hospital, Ranchi.

As Mishra was being wheeled into the Operation theatre, his only thought was for Constable Bunkar and his condition. Bunkar had been with him since long and today he felt morally responsible for the jawan. It was only when his Commandant asked Mishra if he would want to speak to his own family that Mishra remembered his own looming surgery. Mishra had lost his mother when he was only seven; hence he had a very faint memory of her. He now reached out to his younger brother who was with the CISF. A quick explanation and an assurance that the father will be informed later; Mishra was now into the surgery. When he regained consciousness, he learnt that Bunkar had been airlifted to Delhi for better management. While the medical officers and experts tried their best, Bunkar succumbed to his injuries. The brave jawan had made the supreme sacrifice at the altar of duty.

Mishra continued to be in the Intensive Care Unit of Apollo, Ranchi for 45 days. The blood loss had been immense and the body took time to heal from the five bullet injuries it had sustained. The trauma of being carried on a makeshift stretcher practically running all the way to the airfield had taken its toll. Mishra was then shifted to the CRPF Centre in Ranchi where he regained his strength and vitality.

Prakash Ranjan Mishra was awarded the Shaurya Chakra on the occasion of Independence Day, 2013. He had already been conferred with the Second Bar to Gallantry earlier that year. His leadership, gallantry and presence of mind under adversity combined with his acumen and operational efficiency has ensured that the CRPF personnel have kept the naxal menace at bay. For Mishra, Gallantry is a way of life.

□

Our Gallant Heroes

SL. NO.	FORCE IRLA NO.	RANK	NAME	UNIT	YEAR	MEDAL
1	943040199	CT/GD(M)	LATE KAMLESH KUMARI	088 BN	2002	ASHOK CHAKRA (POSTH)
2	710351525	CT/GD	LATE T. MOHANAN	035 BN	1988	VIR CHAKRA (POSTH)
3	041732922	CT/GD	LATE BHRIGUNANDAN CHOUDHARY(POSTH)	205 CoBRA	2014	KIRTI CHAKRA (POSTH)
4	4705	COMDT	SHAHEED PRAMOD KUMAR	49 Bn	2017	KIRTI CHAKRA (POSTH)
5	4685	COMDT	SHRI CHETAN KUMAR CHEETA	45 Bn	2017	KIRTI CHAKRA
6	065044856	CT/GD	SHAHEED PRADIP KUMAR PANDA	132 Bn	2019	KIRTI CHAKRA (POSTH)
7	155110491	CT/GD	SHAHEED RAJENDRA KUMAR NAIN	130 Bn	2019	KIRTI CHAKRA (POSTH)
8	6678	DC (Now 2-I/C)	SHRI HARSHPAL SINGH	06/111 BN	2019	KIRTI CHAKRA
9	850787618	HC/GD	SHRI Y. B. THAPA	023 BN	2002	SHAURYA CHAKRA
10	005140022	CT/GD	SHRI D. SANTOSH KUMAR	023 BN	2002	SHAURYA CHAKRA
11	903056294	CT/GD	SHRI SUKHWINDER SINGH	023 BN	2002	SHAURYA CHAKRA
12	901341541	CT/GD	SHRI SHYAMBIR SINGH	SDG	2002	SHAURYA CHAKRA

SL. NO.	FORCE IRLA NO.	RANK	NAME	UNIT	YEAR	MEDAL
13		AIG	SHRI N.M.S. NAIR	SPG	2002	SHAURYA CHAKRA
14	801290395	HC/GD	SHRI CHHOTE LAL	93 BN	2005	SHAURYA CHAKRA
15	5459	A/C	SHRI VIZETO TINYI	33 BN	2006	SHAURYA CHAKRA
16	850832915	HC/GD	SHRI DHARAMBIR SINGH	33 BN	2006	SHAURYA CHAKRA
17	060811911	CT/GD	LATE ASHISH KR TIWARY	202 CoBRA	2011	SHAURYA CHAKRA (POSTH)
18	6123	A/C	SHRI R.K. SINGH	133 BN	2012	SHAURYA CHAKRA
19	7891	A/C	SHRI NAGENDRA SINGH	207 CoBRA	2012	SHAURYA CHAKRA
20	8071	A/C	SHRI VINOJ P. JOSEPH	207 CoBRA	2012	SHAURYA CHAKRA
21	5515	DC	SHRI P.R. MISHRA	203 CoBRA	2013	SHAURYA CHAKRA
22	5005	2-I/C	SHRI HIRA KUMAR JHA	07 BN	2015	SHAURYA CHAKRA (POSTH)
23	9056	AC	SHRI CHANDAN KUMAR	205 CoBRA/101 RAF	2017	SHAURYA CHAKRA
24	060810727	CT/GD	SHRI AMAR NATH MISHRA	205 CoBRA	2017	SHAURYA CHAKRA
25	9780	AC	SHRI VIKASH JAKHAR	209 CoBRA	2018	SHAURYA CHAKRA

SL. NO.	FORCE IRLA NO.	RANK	NAME	UNIT	YEAR	MEDAL
26	121180026	SI	MD. RIYAZ ALAM ANSARI	209 CoBRA	2018	SHAURYA CHAKRA
27	005210466	HC/GD	SHAHEED DHANAWADE RAVINDRA BABAN	182 Bn	2018	SHAURYA CHAKRA (POSTH)
28	6671	DC	SHRI KULDEEP SINGH CHAHAR	182 Bn	2018	SHAURYA CHAKRA
29	880901236	HC/GD	SHRI A.S. KRISHNA	45 Bn	2018	SHAURYA CHAKRA
30	145033655	CT/GD	SHRI K. DINESH RAJA	45 Bn	2018	SHAURYA CHAKRA
31	110049648	CT/GD	SHRI PRAFULLA KUMAR	45 Bn	2018	SHAURYA CHAKRA
32	11159	AC	SHRI ZILE SINGH	180 Bn	2019	SHAURYA CHAKRA
33	145072883	CT/GD	SHRI ZAKER HUSSAIN	06 BN	2019	SHAURYA CHAKRA
34	065211038	CT/GD	SHRI SABLE DNYANESHWAR SHRIRAM	53 BN	2019	SHAURYA CHAKRA

□□□